THE ASSIGNMENT

Darrius Jerome Gourdine

DJG

Enterprises

THE ASSIGNMENT

Darrius Jerome Gourdine,
DJG Enterprises

Cover Design: Paul Woodruff

Book layout and design: Norman Rich

Author photography by James McDuff Photography

For book signings and speaking engagements, send all inquiries to darrius@iamassigned.com.

All scriptural references are taken from the New King James version of the Holy Bible.

www.iamassigned.com

ISBN: 978-0-9755660-5-3

"Be not forgetful to entertain strangers: for thereby some have entertained angels unawares."

— Hebrews 12:2 (KJV)

Today started off just as any other day... any other Wednesday that is.

One thing I hate about Wednesdays is the midweek meetings. I know I'm not the only one on the team who feels these meetings are redundant and unnecessary. We spend well over an hour on Monday going over goals for the week. We spend another hour on Friday going over what goals for the week we actually did achieve. We spend almost three hours on Wednesday talking about the stage of the project we are currently in. I've often wanted to blurt out to my boss that we'd be able to get much further along if we didn't sit in a conference room and spend almost three hours talking about what we just spoke about on Monday and are about to speak about on Friday. To make matters worse, we arrive at the office an hour early for the midweek meeting.

I hate rainy mornings too. Today is a cold and dreary day. It's a bad combination overall. Yet, I have to make the most of it. At least I have something to look forward to this evening. One of my fraternity brothers is in town on business and we'll get together for dinner. I always enjoy seeing friends from college as I usually don't get to see them until homecoming. This will be a welcomed break from the normal Wednesday evening where there isn't a football or basketball game on that I want to see.

As I get into my car and start it, I hear ESPN radio loudly coming through my radio. Apparently I left the volume up when I got out of the car last night. At the same time, my phone vibrates in my pocket. I take the phone out of my pocket as I put my seat belt around my chest and adjust it. I notice that I received a text from my intern Julian.

"Hey Len. Good morning. Meeting for this morning is canceled."

What? So I literally could've stayed in bed another 30 minutes at least? I immediately text back as I drive out of the parking garage of my complex.

"The meeting is canceled? Are you kidding me?"

"Yup! We all coulda stayed in bed another thirty! SMH! LMAO!!"

I like my intern. He knows me so well. I was opposed to a male intern at first as the previous two interns I have had were female. Not that I was interested in a dating scenario with them. I keep my business life and my professional life completely separate. I just tend to get along with women better in my working environment. Julian however knows me well. He knows my patterns. He knows what I order at Starbucks. He knows that I would prefer 30 more minutes of sleep. I laugh as I text him back.

"LOL!! You right! Okay so let's do this. Do me a favor and get the files for the McKenzie project. We might as wel..."

Why is there a flashlight in my eyes?

"We gotta cut him out! We need the saw to cut him out! There's gas on the ground!"

"Get the saw! Bring the saw!"

What's happening? What's going on? I can't see past this flashlight in my face... I'm sleepy but my body hurts all over! I hear voices! People screaming! Sirens!

"Okay don't cut near his head! The sparks will fly off and may burn him!"

"Hurry up! He's lost a lot of blood!"

I can't move to see what all the commotion is over. I'm so sleepy.

"He's gonna need an immediate transfusion as soon as we get there! He's lost a lot of blood! I'm starting the..."

Where am I?

"I don't think he's gonna ma..."

What is happening!

I'm falling! Falling! Fire! Everywhere! My arms and legs are on fire! My face is on fire! I put my hands over my face and it's all on fire! What just happened to me! Am I in Hell? Hell is real? I'm burning!

There's fire everywhere! There are people everywhere! Everyone is screaming! It stinks horribly! I've never felt this kind of pain! How can I get out of here! This isn't supposed to happen to me! What did I do to deserve this?

Someone grabs me and I turn to see who it is. In the midst of my incredible pain and burning, I see that it is a monster! He is on fire too but he grabs me and throws me down! I hit the ground and he jumps on top of me. He starts punching me with fiery fists! The ground is wet but the liquid is so incredibly hot that it burns my back.

Get off me! Leave me alone! Get off me!

I try to get away but another monster jumps on me! I now see that these monsters are everywhere and they are beating up people all around me! Everyone is on fire... burning... and screaming... and yelling! Please help me! Stop this! Stop! Stop! Stop!

I immediately sit up and scream. My body is wet with sweat! My room is completely dark other than the moonlight creeping through my shades and making lines on the hard wood floor of my bedroom. I'm breathing heavy and I quickly take both my hands and feel my body. I'm not on fire. I look left, right, left and right again and make sure there are no monsters, screaming people or fire around me! It was a dream! It was the absolute worse dream I have ever had.

I close my eyes and take in a huge breath. As I exhale, I lean over to my nightstand and turn on the light. As soon as the light illuminates the room, I see a man standing by my window. There is another man sitting in my reading chair close to him.

The sight of these two men scares me to the point where I feel my heart in my throat. I then notice a third man standing at my bedroom door.

"What the Hell! Who are you! What the Hell are you doing here?"

"Interesting choice of words. Turn the lights on." he says.

"What! Who are you! Who are you!" I scream.

I'm scared out of my mind and I'm screaming at this man sitting in my bedroom. Before I can comprehend what he said to me, my lights turn on. The three men are all wearing blue suits, white shirts and different color ties. This startles me so much that I fall out of my bed and onto the floor. I scramble to my feet as quickly as I can while holding the blanket up to cover my bare chest.

"Who are you! What are you doing in my apartment!"

The seated man is the only one sitting. The other two are standing by the window and by the door. The one by the door is the one who turned my lights on. The seated man speaks. "Let me explain what's going on and who we are. Please sit down on your bed. We're not here to hurt you."

I remain standing holding my blanket against my body like it is a bullet proof vest.

"I need to explain the dream you just had. You were falling and when you landed, there was fire all around... like you were in Hell."

The seated man has described my dream! What in the world is going on?

"How did you... what is going on here! Is this some kind of joke or something?"

"Please have a seat and I can explain everything."

I'm still standing.

"I know this is unorthodox Len but if you..."

"How do you know my name?"

The man uncrosses his legs and leans forward. Both his elbows are now resting on his legs and he looks me directly into my eyes. His stare is ice cold as he begins to speak. "Your name is Lendall King Williams. You were born February 7th, 1979 to Frederick James Williams and Geraldine Elizabeth Nelson. Your older sister is Lisa. Your younger brother is Frederick Jr. Your brother's wife is Allison. Your parents think you'll never get married."

"Stop! How do you know all of this about me!"

The man leans back in his chair. "Sit down and I'll explain."

He hasn't taken his eyes off of me once. I look at the other two men who are both staring at me. One by the door, the other by the window. Neither of them has said a word. I slowly sit on the edge of my bed.

"Thank you." the man says. "Just so you aren't startled or frightened, I'm going to have Kevin take a shirt out of your closet to give to you to put on. Like I said, we aren't going to hurt you. I need to explain who we are and what just happened to you."

Without waiting for my approval, the man by the door steps into my walk-in closet.

"My name is Alexander. This is Josh and the man in your closet as I said is Kevin. My job is to explain what just happened to you and help you navigate through a very important decision that you have to make."

"Decision?"

Kevin throws a shirt toward me that lands next to me on the bed. I'm still in a state of shock, fear and disbelief. I don't even pick up the shirt.

"Len, I understand this is all very troubling. Put your shirt on and I promise I will explain everything. It will all make sense. Won't be an easy pill to swallow, but I'll do my best to make it understandable."

Kevin has reappeared from my closet. He is holding a pair of pants. He tosses them on the bed as well. I pick up the shirt and put it on. "Okay. Talk."

"Okay. You were involved in a terrible car accident. You were paying attention to your phone and not on the road and you slammed into another car. The momentum of that car spun your car into oncoming traffic and your car was obliterated. By the time rescue workers got to you, you were bleeding profusely. You had to be cut from the vehicle and were in and out of consciousness."

"What!"

"Yes. That's what happened to you yesterday."

"Then... how...

"How are you here now in your bedroom without a bruise or a scratch?"

I don't know how to respond to his question. This makes no sense. If I had a car accident yesterday as bad as he is describing, why am I not in a hospital? How did I end up in my bed with nothing on but my shorts? Who are these men and how did they get into my room, in this high rise, past the doorman?

"Len, you died in the ambulance on the way to the hospital. You didn't make it."

"Wait... what!"

He continues speaking as if he never heard me. "You died and your soul went to Hell. What you experienced wasn't a bad dream or a nightmare. It was real. Hell is real. Heaven is real. Based on the way you lived your life before death, you were judged and sentenced to eternity in Hell."

I open my mouth but nothing comes out. No words. Not even a breath. I don't know what to say. This has to be some sort of practical joke. This will absolutely go down as the greatest practical joke of the century.

Alexander continues. "Once a person is sentenced to Hell, their soul immediately is transported. You feel like you're falling. A continuous drop that scares you. Scares the living daylights out of you. When you hit the ground, you're burning. The fire is so intense. You've never felt fire so painful. You had a few demons jump on you and they began to beat you. You felt a hot liquid like lava. That's called brimstone. Am I adequately describing what happened in what you thought was a dream?"

"Ye... yes... but how do you know all this?"

"My job is to inform you of what just happened to you and to instruct you on what to do next. Kevin and Josh are only here as a security measure. There are people who have a hard time handling what I am telling them and they need to be subdued. So far, it seems like you're not one of those cases. That works in your favor. You don't want to be handled by Josh or Kevin."

Neither Josh or Kevin say a word or even move a muscle.

"Now that I've told you what happened to you, let me explain why you're back in your bed and what happens now."

"Yes please because all I want to do at this point is lay back down and wake up tomorrow like none of this actually happened."

"You spent a few moments in Hell in order to have a recollection of it. The human mind can easily record events. Documentation is built into the framework of the mind. Humans however have a much stronger sense of memory when it comes to the sense of touch. If you feel something, you would have a much greater chance of remembering what you felt than the day you felt it if 15 years go by. So, you were cast into Hell and now can easily and readily remember what it feels like to be there. You now have a decision to make."

"So... you're trying to tell me that I was in a car accident. I died. I went to Hell. I'm now back in my room with no evidence of a car accident. No bruises. No broken bones. Not even a busted lip. You three guys break into my place and tell me this ridiculous story and I'm supposed to believe this?"

"Yes. You have to."

"Okay well how about this! I don't have to believe a damn thing! I don't know who you are or how you got in here but I'm calling the police!"

Immediately Josh and Kevin walk toward the bed where

I'm seated. Alexander simply watches. I jump out of the bed and back up into my nightstand. My lamp falls and crashes on the floor. I frantically back up to the wall as they come toward me.

"Get away from me! Get out! Get out!"

Kevin walks across the bed to get to me. Josh walks on the side of the bed where I am. They have me cornered. I don't know what they plan to do other than rob me.

In a desperate attempt to escape, I jump onto the bed and hope to get past Kevin. I don't. Both Kevin and Josh are big men. Much bigger than Alexander or myself. Kevin smothers me and Josh quickly joins him. They are trying to pin me down as I am screaming for help.

"Help! Somebody help me! Help! Get off me! Let me go! Help!"

Kevin is on top of me as Josh pulls my arm. He takes my wrist and pins it down onto the bed. I see out of the corner of my eye that Alexander has stood up and is calmly walking toward the three of us on the bed.

"Len, as I explained, this news isn't easy to swallow or believe. We all get that. Unfortunately, it is our truth and now your truth too. It has become rather customary to do this to prove the authenticity of our claim."

As hard as I'm fighting, Kevin is a huge man and is holding me down easily. Josh, another man that outweighs me easily is holding my left arm out. My screams mean nothing to them.

"This is a small reminder of what Hell feels like. I'm only going to do this for a second."

Alexander does something to my arm that burns like a burn I've never felt before. I let out a scream and he stops. Tears well up in my eyes and I can feel my heart beating in my chest. I begin coughing like I'm going to choke and Josh lets go of my arm. Kevin eases up off me and I grab my throat to try to breathe normally. I'm coughing hard and now curled in the fetal position.

I've never been so afraid in my life! What in the world is happening to me? Why me? Why now? This cannot be real! This cannot be happening! Who are these people and why did they choose me!

"Len! Len! You have to breathe in your nose and out through your mouth! Breathe Len! Breathe!"

As crazy as this day has been, I have no other choice but to listen to Alexander and try to breathe. As he has instructed, inhaling through my nose and out through my mouth starts to calm me. I immediately look at my arm which is still hot. There is no scarring or melted skin. No bruise or scratches. Yet I absolutely feel the pain that he just inflicted, even though it is decreasing.

"What are you doing to me? Why are you doing this to me?"

"My job is to explain this to you. If you fight, I remind you of what Hell feels like. That's what I just did to your arm. If you continue to fight this, I can send you back to Hell and we can end this whole thing right now. You can go back to Hell with no choice or option. Or you can stay here and hear me out."

I don't know what to say. Whatever Alexander just did to my arm was very real. I still feel it. The pain was so intense it made me cry and start to convulse. I never want to feel that pain or be reminded of it again.

Josh and Kevin slowly retreat back to the positions they were in previous. Josh goes back to standing by the window and Kevin by the door. Alexander is standing at the side of the bed where I am still seated. I'm just recovering from whatever he just did to my arm and from these huge men overpowering me. I sit up and lean my back against the headboard. They have my attention. I'm listening. I'm frightened out of my mind. My body won't stop shaking. They have my attention.

"I know this all sounds crazy. It was when I first heard it as well. This is not a dream and we didn't break in here. We're here on assignment and this is what we do. We inform people of the world they have to adjust to after death. We let them know of the awful consequence that awaits. We train them and make sure they stay on course for what they're supposed to do."

"What does all that mean?"

"You died in that car accident. Based on the way you lived your life, you were sentenced to spend eternity in Hell. You can delay your fate though if you choose to work with us."

"Work with you? Who are you?"

"We are members of The Agency. We are a disciplined organization with members all over the world. My job is to help train and mentor you. I am to prepare you for your new life and begin to build you for your assignment."

"My what?"

"Guys. I think I'm good." Alexander motions to Josh and Kevin and without ever speaking a word, both walk out of my bedroom. He turns back to me. "I believe we can talk now without any type of outburst from you."

Alexander stands and walks back to the chair he was originally seated in. He continues as he sits back down. "When a person dies and is sentenced to Hell, they may get the option of working for The Agency until such a time that there sentence must be served. You have been selected and are fortunate enough to have that option. Some are fortunate, most aren't. As a word of advice, don't squander your good fortune."

"What does working for the agency mean? What agency? What do I have to do?"

"I know you have a lot of questions and I can answer a few now. The bulk of your questions will be answered starting tomorrow. I'm going to drive you to an address downtown. We have to be there by 9:00 am for orientation. There will be a question and answer period during the session."

"Orientation? Are you serious?"

"Very."

This is unbelievable! Orientation? What is this that I've been placed into? I have to go to an orientation? Like a new job?"

"It's a training. Extensive training. It begins tomorrow. There will be others that will be starting in tomorrow's session with you. A lot of your questions will be answered then."

"How many other people? They all in the same boat as me?"

"Six hundred and sixty six. That's the size of every incoming class."

"Six hundred and sixty six! What? That many people died yesterday?"

"No." Alexander takes his phone out of his pocket and looks at it before he continues. "Yesterday there were 147,896 deaths. Out of that number, 666 were selected for The Agency. From that number, an average of roughly 47.6 can't handle the emotional pressure. That leaves a little over 610 individuals per day added to our cause."

My head is spinning. Now I have a million questions and I don't know which of the million should be the first.

"You have over 600 people every day that join your organization? Every day?"

"Yes. We are the world's largest organization. We are very well managed. Very organized. Very disciplined."

"What is your purpose? Why am I a part of this and what am I supposed to do?"

"I actually don't know that part. I don't know what your assignment is going to be. That information, you will receive at a later date. For now, you need to get rest and be ready to leave by 8:30 tomorrow morning. I'll be back to pick you up."

"You're leaving me here? By myself?"

"No. Josh and Kevin are downstairs. You're not allowed to leave the building. They're here to make sure you're here at 8:30 tomorrow when I get back. Your communication devices have been taken so you have no means to reach out to family or friends. Even if you did, they wouldn't recognize you. In their hearts and minds, you're dead. You'll learn why they cannot recognize you in the days to come."

I sit in silence as Alexander stands up. He buttons his sport coat.

"You're going to have a lot going through your mind. That happens to everyone. When you lay down, it will seem as if you cannot fall asleep but you will. You're going to probably dream about Hell. Our minds work that way. You're going to wake up tomorrow and pray to God that today was a dream. Then you will hear me knocking on your door to take you to orientation. You're going to have to get up. You don't want to suffer the consequences of being late."

He turns to leave the room and opens my bedroom door.

"Wait!"

He turns back to me and speaks before I ask the question at the forefront of my mind. "Yes this is real. This is totally real. Unfortunately, this is your new normal and is my total reality. You have a ton of questions. Everyone does. There will be a lengthy question and answer period tomorrow when you can have all your questions answered."

With no more words, he walks out of my bedroom door. I hear his footstep on each step from my second floor to my first floor, across the hardwood floor of my condo, then out the door. I hear the door lock as if he has a key to my place. How did Alexander get a key to my place?

I jump out of bed and run to my bedroom window. I look outside to see if I see Alexander exit the building. My bedroom window faces the front of the condominium that I live in. After a few minutes, I see him walk out. He gets into a white SUV parked across the street from my building. I see the light of his cell phone illuminate the inside of his truck once he is seated. I can see his silhouette as he fastens his seat belt. He takes a moment to talk on his phone before starting his vehicle, pulling out of the parking spot and driving into the night. I run to the bedroom door, open it and take to the stairs. Quickly I get to the bottom step and to my condo door. It is locked.

Pausing for a moment, I consider what Alexander told me. Josh and Kevin are downstairs. He also told me that I have no communication devices. I consider running downstairs to see if they're really down there but first... my phone! Where is my phone? I begin to search my condo. My kitchen drawers. The living room area. All of my furniture is as I left it when I went to work. Flat screen TV on the wall but I don't see the remote. I keep the remote in the same place every day. I rummage through my place looking for my phone and now for the remote. Nothing. I run back up to my bedroom and search in there. Nothing.

Should I go back downstairs? If I go downstairs and those two big guys aren't there, then maybe this is all one big dream and I can wake up and go to work. No one would believe how real this dream is though! If this is a prank, this is the best prank ever! Who would go through such lengths to pull this kind of prank? I got crazy frat brothers but this is extreme! And what in the world did he do to my arm! That was real!

I stand in silence for a moment and remember Lawrence, my next door neighbor. He and his wife Alicia are home. They're probably sleep. They moved into the condo next to mine one month after I moved in. We've watched a few basketball games together. If I can't go down to the lobby and leave the building, at least I can use Lawrence's phone.

I run back down my stairs to my door and open it. As I fling the door open, Josh is standing in the hall staring at me. He shocks me and my heart drops. He speaks to me for the first time.

"Don't consider speaking to Lawrence or any of your other neighbors." He says. "We knew you would try that. Go back inside and get some rest. You're gonna need it."

I'm too stunned to move. I can't say anything. I'm in a state of silent shock. He then steps toward me which snaps me out of my shocked state. I jump backward fearing he will try to hurt me. He instead grabs my door and slowly closes it. He leaves me on the inside and himself out in the hall. If nothing else, he has proven Alexander's words to be true. He and Josh are indeed not allowing me to leave the building.

I don't have a choice. I don't have an idea of what to do. They suggested I get sleep but I have no idea how that can happen based on what I've been told. My body is exhausted. My arm still hurts from what they did. My mind is racing. I don't believe I'll be able to sleep. Yet I walk back upstairs to my bedroom. I'm now walking a lot slower than I was when I was looking for my phone and remote.

I stop by my bathroom and turn on the light. I stare at myself in the mirror. How am I dead? What if I see my mother tomorrow? I can easily run into my coworkers. What about Lawrence? He leaves for work about the same time I do. What if I see him or his wife tomorrow morning? Won't they all recognize me as alive? I turn on the cold water and splash it on my face. I put cold water on my arm and feel no relief. Still painful.

I decide to lay down. What other choice do I have?

There's fire all around me! Burning me! Burning everyone around me! This is incredibly painful! I'm screaming and trying to rub the fire off my body. A monster grabs me and throws me down a hill. The hill is on fire and I slide through it, burning as I go down. I scream at the top of my lungs as I reach the bottom of the hill and slide into a flowing lake. The lake is red and on fire. I bump into two men and a woman who are also screaming and on fire. One of the men shoves me aside and I fall further into the lake. The lake is hotter than the flames and I notice a lot of people trying to climb out of it a get back to the hill. The undercurrent is so heavy, it's hard to not be swept away. People crawling all over each other to get out of it. I scream and some of the liquid goes into my mouth. I've never felt something so hot enter my mouth. My tongue is on fire and I start to choke and scream simultaneously. As the fire descends down my throat a monster grabs me by my face.

I sit up in my bed and grab my face immediately. I'm breathing heavy and looking around my dark room. I'm alone. It's dark. It's dark outside. I look at my alarm clock next to me. It's 4:47 am. I had fallen asleep. I don't remember feeling tired. I remember getting in the bed and staring at the ceiling. I don't remember falling asleep. My mind was racing and I thought I wouldn't be able to fall asleep. I feel trapped.

Alexander warned me that I would fall asleep. He warned me that I would dream about Hell. Both have happened and I have four hours before he's coming to get me. This is the worst torture imaginable. Waiting to find out what happens next. Hoping this is some weird prank that has gone too far. Wanting to wake up in this very bed and put all of this behind me. Remembering the pain of fire. The ugly beings jumping all over me. The other people screaming and scrambling all over one another.

I get out of the bed and look out of my window. The parking spot where Alexander's SUV was parked is now occupied by a small car. The street is quiet. My room is quiet. I turn and look at my bed. I'm hesitant to get into it for fear of dreaming again. I hate that dream. I hate that place. I don't want to go there. I don't have a choice. Now I do feel tired and drained. My mind is still racing with questions, thoughts and images of what I saw. Still hard to believe what Alexander said. Right now, I'm forced to believe him. My only other option would be to try to escape and face Josh and Kevin who seem to be keeping me hostage. They are both large men. I'd be no match for them physically. I've never owned a gun. If I did, I'm sure they would have found it and gotten rid of it like they did with all of my electronic devices.

I climb back into my bed but don't lay down. I sit up and cry. I can't believe this is happening to me and I don't know what to do. I have no way to prove what these guys are saying is right. I do have the pain that I absolutely felt in my arm. I never want to feel that again. If what Alexander said is true, then I'm doomed and in a horrible situation.

I lay my head back and stare at the ceiling. In this moment, all I can think of doing is praying for myself. I've never been much of a person to pray. I have before. Everyone has prayed at least once or twice but I never formally joined any church. I've been to church before. I grew up in Catholic school so I attended church service with my classmates all the time. I even was an altar boy before. Once I graduated and went to high school, attending mass was no longer a requirement so I never went. I remember dating a woman in college who went to church and I went with her a few times. Her church was much different than what I had seen in Catholic school. The music was a lot louder. The people danced and screamed at times. She asked me if I enjoyed it afterward and I said yes but I can't honestly admit that I did. I wasn't sure what was going on for most of it and I never went back. I find myself now searching for words to say for God to help me. Can he help me? I don't know.

"Please... God... help me."

With tears running out of my eyes, this is all I can muster. I turn onto my side and curl into the fetal position. My tears convert into a full cry as I try to wake up from this incredible nightmare.

I hear the knock on the door as if I had knocked myself. Somehow Alexander must have gotten the keys to my condo. He is on the other side of my bedroom door knocking. That means he walked into the condo, up the stairs, and to my room. Not sure why he doesn't come in. If he is able to get into the condo, I'm sure he is able to get into the bedroom.

"Len. It's Alexander. I'm coming in."

Wow, a polite Grim Reaper.

The door opens and Alexander sees me curled in my bed. I wanted to get up. I wanted to wake up to this being a dream. I don't think I went to sleep. This has been the longest night I have ever lived through.

"I can't believe you asked before you came in."

"My role, which you'll understand later, is to help you transition from your previous life to the afterlife. The easier you can make that transition, the better it is for you and me. I can provide as much comfort as I can but the truth is, it's a bad situation. You can make the best of it or give up and go back."

I pop up in bed with tears in my eyes once again. I thought I had cried my tear ducts out but apparently I haven't. "So this is really real? This ain't a prank or something! Come on! Jokes over!"

"No, It's not a joke. You have twenty minutes. Either you get up, get in the shower, and get dressed or you go back to the pit. That dream you had last night wasn't a dream. It was a revisit as a reminder of what awaits.

There are millions of souls there now wishing they had the opportunity you have. If you can delay that dreadful place for thirty more seconds, it would be the best thirty seconds you will ever spend. So make up your mind now. Right now."

His stare can penetrate a solid brick wall. He silently awaits my answer.

"Okay. I'm getting up. Um, is there something specific I'm supposed to wear or bring?"

"Dress as if you were going to work today. I'll be waiting downstairs. Don't be late."

Alexander turns and closes my bedroom door as he walks out. I wipe my eyes and place both hands over my face. My elbows are resting on my knees. My feet are flat on the floor as I sit on the side of the bed. In another moment, I stand up. I'm so weak emotionally that I stumble back onto the bed. I make myself stand to my feet and steady myself. I walk into the bathroom to get ready.

Alexander is seated at my breakfast table with a tablet in his hand. Josh and Kevin are seated as well.

"Good morning." Josh speaks to me as I come down the stairs.

"Um. Good morning." I respond. Kevin simply nods.

"Alright, let's get a move on. Not sure about traffic going downtown this morning." Alexander says as he turns his tablet off.

"Where are we going?" I ask.

"Today is orientation. It's at a building downtown. Like I said, you will have most of your questions answered today when we get there. They have food provided as well so don't worry about breakfast."

"What? Food provided? Are you serious?"

"We have to eat don't we?" Alexander nudges Kevin on the arm and they both laugh as the three stand up.

I follow Alexander and Kevin who walk out of the condo in front of me and Josh behind me. We step onto the elevator and go down to the first floor. No words are spoken as we go from my penthouse level down to the first floor. As the doors open, I see my neighbor Lawrence at his mailbox. I immediately want to scream his name so he can possibly help me. Lawrence turns around as he is locking his mailbox. He locks eyes with me and then notices the three men I'm with.

"Hey Alexander. What's up fellas?" Lawrence says.

"Morning Lawrence." Alexander responds.

I look at Alexander who just spoke to Lawrence. I quickly glance back at Lawrence, then back to Alexander. "You know him?" I shockingly ask Alexander.

"Yes. Lawrence has been with The Agency for four years now."

I'm so stunned that I stop walking and stare at Lawrence who walks past and smiles at me. It's almost like my feelings of shock and horror don't matter. Josh pushes me to keep walking and we exit the building. Now my head is truly spinning as I consider all the times I have spent with Lawrence. He has been on this assignment for four years? I haven't known him for four years. Does that mean that he too died and is living in this alternate existence?

I'm completely overwhelmed and my knees buckle as I step outside of the building. I think I'm going to hit the ground and pass out but Kevin catches me as I almost tumble into Alexander. Josh grabs my free arm and helps to stabilize me. The doorman of my condominium rushes to help. He tries to help Josh and Kevin bring me to my feet. Josh and Kevin are both huge men and can easily pick up a small man like me. Steven, the doorman, recognizes that his assistance isn't needed but asks if I am OK.

"You okay Brian?" Steven asks.

Brian? Who is Brian? I look at Steven with a weird look on my face as I'm not sure who he is talking to. Before I can question him, Alexander speaks.

"He's fine. Late night with the fellas. You know how

it gets when the game runs late but the bar stays open."
Alexander laughs which causes Steven to laugh as well. I'm
back on my feet... still confused... still wobbly.

"Yeah! What a game! Double overtime! Did you see that
shot that won it?" Steven asks.

"Listen, people used to say Michael Jordan was the best
player in the league. Then they said LeBron James. But tell
me if Clifton Burgess isn't the best player you've ever seen!"
Alexander responds.

"Better than LeBron James? Come on man!" Steven says
laughing.

As the conversation shifts to professional basketball,
Kevin walks to the SUV that I saw Alexander getting into
last night. He starts it and pulls out of the parking spot. As
he pulls to the front walkway of my building, Steven opens
the back door.

"He may not have the strength of LeBron or the finesse of
Jordan but look at his shooting percentage and how young
he is. Give him the same amount of years as the two of them
and he will dominate!" Alexander says as he walks around
the SUV to get into the passenger seat. Josh nudges me to
get into the backseat with him.

Steven laughs. "Yeah, we'll see! Have a great day Brian,
hope you feel better buddy!" Steven closes the door to the
SUV after Josh and I get in. Steven calls everyone buddy.
I have heard him say that from the day I moved into this
luxury condo on the outskirt of town. I normally don't go
in and out of the front door since I own a parking spot in
our garage. Occasionally I would step outside of the main

door in the lobby to say hello when I checked my mail. We too have talked basketball. Steven is a nice guy. Still unsure who he was referring to when he said the name Brian.

"Um..." I begin to ask and Alexander interrupts me to answer my question before I ask it.

"Brian is your name now. You would've been told that today in training but Steven beat us to it. He doesn't know you as Len. He knows you as Brian."

"But..."

"You don't look the same to him. When you look in the mirror, you see the Len you've always seen. When he sees you though, he sees another image. You'll learn that in the training today."

"And Lawrence?"

"Lawrence has seen both sides of you. He knew you before you died so he knows Len. Now he sees you with me and immediately knows what happened to you. He's already been through orientation and training so he's well aware of the new life situation."

I look out the window, still trying to make sense of all of this. My mind is racing in a hundred and fifty directions and I cannot figure out which direction is which. I take note that Kevin is driving toward downtown, the exact same direction I drove in for work every day. I was driving in and talking about the ridiculous weekly meetings we had. How I wish I could sit through one of those meetings right now!

I wonder what would happen if I jump out of the truck

and run for my life. I could get someone to help me. Help me get away from these people and get me back to my regular life. If this is an attempt to kidnap me, I don't know who would be behind such a plan or why. I have money but I'm certainly not a billionaire. I could easily cut a sizable check for my freedom and normalcy back. Is that what this is about? How far would I get running from these guys? Josh and Kevin are certainly big men but how fast are they? Since I'm not sitting behind Alexander, it would take him a while to get out and come around the SUV to chase me. With the addition of the morning rush hour traffic, I could probably weave in and out of some cars, make my way across the other side, and get to a back alley between two of the buildings.

"Just so you're prepared for today, there's a few things I want to mention to you before we get there. First of all, don't be alarmed if you see..."

Before Alexander can finish his statement to me, I try to open the door to make a run for it. Much to my surprise and dismay, the back doors to the SUV don't have door handles to open the door. I'm locked in. I recognize that and bang on the window instead. "Help! Somebody help me! Kidnapped! Help me!" Josh slams his forearm across me and takes the wind out of my chest. He's so strong that he pins me back against the seat. I can't move even though I'm fighting with all that is within me. I'm kicking violently against the back of Kevin's seat, trying to get free of Josh's grip. Alexander reaches from the front seat and grabs my leg. He quickly does the same thing to my leg that he did to my arm last night. The burn is so intense that I let out a scream that even scares myself. I try to pull my leg away but Josh has me in a position where I can't go but so far. This time Alexander does the burn thing longer. I can't take it any longer and he stops.

"Listen to me! I know this is very heavy but you're going to make this situation worse for yourself! You have a great opportunity right now to stay on Earth! If you mess this up, you will be taken back today! Why go back today when you can possibly stay for a thousand years! Don't be stupid man!" For the first time, Alexander raises his voice toward me. My leg feels like it is dipped in molten lava and I'm silenced by his words. I can't even form a sentence due to the pain in my leg.

Josh removes his arm from across my chest. I bend down and hold my leg and cry as the pain is so intense, I can barely breathe. I scream out, only because it hurts so badly.

"Breathe... in through your nose and out through your mouth. In... out."

I follow Alexander's breathing instructions and slowly sit back in my seat. I look at Josh who is looking out of the other window, no longer concerned with me. This seems to be routine for he and Kevin. How many times have these guys done this to people? What in the world is this that these guys are doing to me? Where are we going?

This is real. If this were a dream, the pain I felt would have awakened me by now. That felt too real. Both my arm and leg are still in pain. If Hell is anything like the two dreams I had and this pain I feel, I never want to go. I need to find out in this orientation how I can avoid that place forever.

Traffic opens up and Kevin takes us through the heart

of downtown. My office is literally five blocks east of where we're driving now. In the middle of Center Street, he turns into a parking lot filled with cars. I've passed this building before and never knew what it was. The parking lot is large as is the building. There is a gate that has to be opened and a guard sitting in a booth. Kevin pulls a card out of his shirt pocket and holds it up to a sensor which opens the gate. He then waves at the guard as we drive in. The gate closes behind us. Kevin is searching for a parking spot.

"This... this is it?"

"Yes," Alexander says. "This is where your orientation and training will be.

As Kevin pulls into a parking spot, I feel an incredible sense of fear. I feel like my heart is going to leap through my chest and onto the floor of this truck. I almost hear my own heartbeat. I look out the window and see lots of people walking from their cars to the building. Easily over one hundred people walking into the building from the parking lot.

We exit the vehicle and I literally feel my limbs shaking. My teeth feel like they're chattering together. I'm shivering like it's a blizzard outside when in actuality, it's quite a warm day. I'm scared. I'm curious. I'm terrified. I'm hoping this is the most elaborate hoax in human history. I'm hoping that I walk in the door and see all of my friends and family yelling surprise! I want to see balloons, and my mom and my co-workers. I want this to all be a dream or misunderstanding. What I don't want is for what Alexander described to be my new truth.

"All of these people are here for the orientation like me?"

"No." Alexander answers. "You can see them in groups of fours to understand it better. Each person in your shoes has a person like me, like a mentor. There are also two security personnel who assist the mentor in bringing the person in for orientation."

"Oh. So only the terrified looking people are the trainees." Alexander and Josh laugh. I don't think Kevin is paying enough attention to hear what I said.

"Actually, that's exactly correct. People will have a very difficult time coming to the reality of what you're about to be told. I told you yesterday that some people can handle it and some can't. That's entirely up to the person. We make our best attempt to prepare you as much as possible and give you all the information you need to succeed in what you are tasked to do. The Day of Dread may be hundreds of years from now. Do the best you can until you can no longer. But if you can't handle it, we have security in place like Josh here and Kevin who are trained to handle the situation. My role is to deliver the awful news, then help you transition into your life. I have a great success rate so far."

Kevin opens the glass double doors for us to walk through. Alexander walks first, I follow, then Josh and Kevin. We enter a large lobby area where there are seemingly hundreds of people. Most are talking. Some are laughing with one another. I have to assume the people laughing are members of this agency and not people like myself that are just learning of this awful fate. There are people here of every single nationality. White people. Black people. Asian people. Hispanic people. On the left side of the room, there are tables that resemble registration tables at a convention. It brings me back to the early days of my fraternity. The brothers and I would road trip to a convention in a major city. Once there, the registration tables were set up just like these. We could then check in by our last name and receive our convention bag and materials. On the right side of the room seems to be an elaborate display of bagels, breads and coffees. I don't know who could even consider eating at a time like this but surprisingly, people are. I assume, once again, that these are members of the agency partaking in the food.

Alexander leads me toward the registration tables. Just like with the recollection of my fraternity events, there are registration tables according to last names. We stand in the line for last names beginning with the letters W-Z. "I know you're wondering. Wilcox is my last name. Alexander Wilcox."

"So this is a registration?"

"Not so much a registration but a check in. I have to check us in which means I made contact with you, gave you the information, and delivered you to your first day of orientation and training. If I don't do that, you will be unaccounted for and I'd have to answer for that."

Wow, this is serious! No balloons.

"This may be dumb but is there any way to get out of this?"

"No."

I don't ask another question as we wait our turn to sign in. I don't want to sound stupid and I honestly don't want to learn more about this truth. This is an awful fate that I wouldn't wish on my worst enemy. I don't even know all the aspects of it and what it really means but I'm terrified of my dreams and I fear that pain that Alexander put on my arm and leg. I look around the room again and am in awe at the number of people here.

I hear an outburst from behind me.

"No! No! No! Help me!" A woman is screaming behind us. She is standing in the line for last names ending in S-V. As quickly as she screams out, she is grabbed. Some people surrounding her scream as well as they watch two men grab her almost violently. They step aside as they watch this woman who is still screaming and crying. She is wrestled to the floor and subdued. She had to have been sedated because her screams lower instantly. They did something to her that must have put her to sleep. Two of the three men with her pick her up off the floor. The two men follow a third man, I assume her mentor, through the crowd and out a door in the back of this large lobby.

I've decided to not ask any more questions but Alexander fills me in anyway. "Like I said, everyone can't take this. The reality of the situation does set in and some people break. If that happens.... well never mind."

"Well what?" I ask.

Alexander doesn't answer me. Instead, he turns toward the W-Z table. The four people in front of us have just stepped away after signing in. Alexander steps to the table and picks up a pen to sign in. "Hey Marge."

The lady seated at the desk doesn't look up yet responds. "Good morning Alexander. You're in conference room A-16 on the fifteenth floor." She is looking into a small tablet device.

Good morning? Is she serious? For who?

"Thanks." Alexander thanks her as she hands him an object that resembles a long key. "A-16?"

"Yes sir." She goes back to her tablet, never making direct eye contact with me.

Alexander turns away from the table and Josh nudges me to follow. We make our way back away from the line of people. In the time that we were waiting for our room assignment, it seems that a few hundred more people are here. Now the room is much louder. I hadn't even noticed the influx of people or noise. Now I see people crying. Both men and women. I notice an African American man who had to have been a basketball player. He's tall! He must be 6'8 or something. Yet he's crying like a baby with his hands over his face. He's being led to the registration table where we just came from.

Alexander, Josh and Kevin walk across the crowded room as if this is the norm for them. They speak to a few people as we cross the floor of the lobby. A few people shake Alexander's hand. He stops and speaks to a woman for a second before continuing toward the food display.

"As crazy as this may sound, you're gonna have to eat." He says to me.

"Eat? How can I think about food? I'm not hungry at all!"

"You have to. That's one of the reasons this is here. If you don't, you'll be sick within the hour."

"What? Why?"

"Because what you're about to learn is extremely unsettling. The way the human body is set up, you have to have food in your system. In order to keep your digestive system in at least the operational state that it needs to be, you have to eat. Breads are the best thing right now so we have different kinds of breads. Whatever you love, it's all here. Grab whatever you want before we get on the elevators to go up to the fifteenth floor."

I can't believe this. I literally can't believe this. They expect me to eat a bagel so I take the news of being destined to burning in Hell a little better? I'm so afraid of being burned again that at this point, I'd do whatever they say. I have no idea what they did to that lady who screamed out but I honestly don't want to know based on my personal experience with it. If a bagel will prevent me being burned or subdued, I will eat a bagel.

The elevator going up is silent even though it is full of people. I counted four groups if what Alexander said is accurate. Each new trainee has one mentor and two body guards. Sixteen people on the elevator. Of the sixteen, four are here for orientation, ready to learn what this crazy new reality is. The elevator goes up to twenty nine floors. I'm amazed as I've obviously never been in this building before but have certainly passed by it.

We reach the fifteenth floor and are the only ones getting

off. The others are going to floors higher. Kevin holds the door open so Alexander, Josh and I can step out. As we exit the elevator I look back at the people who are still going up. The doors are closing and I make eye contact with an older Asian man. His face looks tired like he hasn't had sleep. His eyes are red. I know he has been crying. His posture is as if he had been punched in the stomach by a prize fighter. He looks defeated. He looks broken. The elevator doors close.

Fear grips me and I'm motionless. The terror of what is coming next is dreadful. The horror of what happens if I resist is overwhelming. I have to walk with them to this orientation or I will face the latter of my fears. I'm not prepared to make that mistake again.

We reach room A-16 and Alexander takes the object he received when we signed in and touches it against the door. There is a beep sound and a red light that I didn't notice. The red light turns green. He opens the door. I walk into a room with a large circular table with a large circle in the middle of it. There are chairs all around the circle. The only break in the circle is to my left where it is open for a person to walk in the middle of the circle. Alexander motions for us to take a seat at the circle. There are already eight people seated at the big circular table. There are also people in the back of the room away from the table, seated and eating. I follow Alexander's leading and take my seat. He sits to my right. On my left, is a gentleman dressed similarly to Alexander. He extends his hand toward me. "Blake. My name is Blake."

"Hey Blake." Alexander speaks to him before I do.

"Alexander, how's it going?" Blake responds.

"It's going."

Blake turns his attention back to me. "What did you say your name was?"

"Um... Len." I say as I sit. My body is shaking so violently from fear that I almost collapse into the chair.

Blake looks past me at Alexander.

"Brian." I had forgotten that my new name is Brian.

Blake leans back so I can see the person he is mentoring. "This is Sheldon. Sheldon this is... Brian, and Alexander."

Sheldon looks at me and opens his mouth. It's clear he is distraught. He doesn't say anything. He tries to say hello but no words come out. Blake puts his arm around Sheldon and squeezes his shoulder with a reassuring squeeze. He then begins to talk in Sheldon's ear.

I look around the room and quickly ascertain that the mentors and trainees are seated around the big circular table. The body guards are all in the back of the room. There are no windows in the room. No clock on the wall. No art work. No podium. No chalkboard. Just a plain room, huge circular table, plenty of chairs.

I hear the beep from the door and it opens. Instead of another four person team coming in to join us, one man walks into the room. He seems young. Definitely younger than Alexander and I. He is carrying a portfolio style briefcase and seems to be in a hurry. Everyone focuses on him as he walks through the one opening in the circular desk. He is now standing in the middle. I glance at the others and I see fear in the eyes of those of us that are trainees. I share their thoughts and terror. I'm hoping that this is the part where this elaborate hoax is revealed.

"Good morning everyone. Before I even introduce myself, let me start by saying... I know this isn't a good morning. You've been briefed by your Chief Presenter about your situation. You couldn't have been told worse news. However, you can make the best of it if you choose to. When I was faced with the same scenario, I chose to make the best of it. I've worked for The Agency for a little over 31 years."

Thirty one years? He died 31 years ago and still works for The Agency?

"If you choose to make the best of this, you can literally put all future thoughts of the dreaded place you dreamed of out of your head. I've developed methods and techniques to do this and I will be sharing those in the next few weeks. Nonetheless, I wanted to share that before I give you my name. So with that, my name is Vince Callahan. I'll be leading you through orientation."

As Vince speaks, he continues to walk within the open circle in the middle of the circular desk. He carefully spins as he walks back and forth to make sure he faces everyone seated. He speaks confidently and addresses each new person with his glance.

"I know you each have a ton of questions and I will get to all of those. Before I do, let me reinforce what your Chief Presenter has expressed to you yesterday and confirm why you're here. Due to a circumstance, the life as you know has

44

ended. Your life was evaluated carefully and judged and it was determined that you would spend the afterlife in the pit of Hell. You were then granted a unique opportunity to...

As Vince is speaking, tears well up in my eyes. Even after Alexander explaining to me and Kevin and Josh detaining me, it starts to become real. It starts to take hold in my heart. That disgusting, painful and vile place that I experienced will be where I end up. Delay it or not, at some point, I will end up there. I begin to cry. Vince clearly sees me crying, yet continues as if I wasn't.

"...process. Through these training classes, you will be educated on many things. How the world operates. How humans think and make decisions. What motivates males versus females. How The Agency is organized. Many things."

Vince walks toward my side of the circular table and places his hand on Alexander's shoulder. "The person that told you of your situation is called the Chief Presenter. His or her job is to present you here for training. They are also tasked at explaining things to you as you progress through your training. You will have contact information for your Chief Presenter starting today."

Another person who is also crying as I am blurts out frantically. "How do I get out of this situation? How can I get out of this?"

Vince turns to address him. "You don't. As your Chief Presenter explained to you, you have one of two options. You can cooperate and work with us or you can meet your destiny right now. If you choose to not work with us, you will be taken away and sent back to Hell. If that is the decision that you make, for whatever reason, understand that there is no turning back. You cannot decide that you can't handle this then change your mind once you get there. It's either here or there. Make a wise decision." Vince takes a moment to look deep into the eyes of each of us seated. Not the Chief Presenters, but the new inductees that are hearing this awful fate for the first time. Nobody dares move. As devastating as this news is, no one is opting to choose the other fate over this one. He has been here for 31 years. I hope to make it that long plus much more if that's possible!

"We provide emotional therapy for each of you. You're going to need it. We understand that this fate, as bad as it is, doesn't compare with how bad the other option is. Based on that logic, we understand that you're going to need to not only accept this but cope with it if you're going to be successful at your assignment. We need a success rate from each incoming class. We manage that through how you process information. You will be evaluated closely as to your understanding of what will be taught you and what your assignment is going to be."

Vince picks up his portfolio which he had placed on top of the circular tablet. He opens it and pulls out folders. He looks at the first one, and hands it to Sheldon, the new inductee seated near me. The second folder is handed to the man who frantically blurted out one minute ago. The third folder is handed to me. The last folder is handed to the only woman inductee in the room. She has been staring into space the entire time we've been sitting here. Her Chief Presenter is a woman.

This is your orientation packet. It contains the information for your new identity and some introductory things that you need to know. I'm going to take the time now to go over it with you. Your Chief Presenter will delve deeper into the packet and provide answers to all of your questions during your one on one time. For now, let's start by opening our packets and beginning with page one.

I look at Alexander who is looking back at me. He has a serious look on his face as he gestures for me to open my packet. I'm almost frozen. I can't believe these people are so detailed as to have typed up a packet with instructions for this. I open the folder and I see my name on the first page.

"You should each see your name on the first page. This is the name that you know of yourself. It is how you have been identified for the amount of years that you lived your beforelife. The afterlife however is different." Vincent says. "You have a new name and a different look. Now don't go looking at yourself or grabbing for a mirror."

A few of the security guys in the back laugh at Vincent's comment.

"You look like yourself to you. When you look in a mirror, you will see the you that you have always seen. When others see you, they will see a different you. No one that you knew in your beforelife will recognize you. Let's read the first page. I'll read the first paragraph and then I will call upon each of you to continue." Vince pauses before he continues. "I... and you see your name from the beforelife... have been selected to accept an assignment from The Agency. I agree to fulfill my assignment to the best of my ability. Should I need help in completing my assignment, I will immediately inform my Chief Presenter and others who have been placed in positions of assistance."

Vince stops reading so we look up at him. He motions toward me. "Why don't you continue with the next paragraph? Read it out loud.

This is torture. You're telling me about the most awful predicament any human can find him or herself in. You're explaining it as if it's a normal occurrence. Yet you're treating me as if I've just been hired by a firm. Now you want me to read, out loud, the most painful thing I've ever gone though.

"Um... my continuation with The Agency is solely based on compliance. Should I choose to be non-compliant toward my assignment or any directives given about my assignment, my agreement with The Agency will be terminated immediately. In case of such an event, I will be transferred back to Hell to endure my total fate.

"Thank you Brian." Vince thanks me. It takes me a moment to recognize that he's speaking to me. I haven't made a name adjustment in my mind yet. "Sheldon, read the next part."

Sheldon doesn't say anything. The moment of silence causes everyone in the room to look in his direction. He's looking down at the paper but not making a sound. His Chief Presenter nudges him.

"Sheldon..." Vince says his name in a serious tone.

My... a... assignment... was selected... specifically... for me." Sheldon pauses.

"Continue."

"I cannot... ask... for... a different... assi... assignment. Based on... nineteen..."

Sheldon pauses again.

Vince, who is reading along with his own paper in his hand, puts his packet on the table. He addresses Sheldon directly. "Sheldon, if you're having a difficult time dealing with this, you can choose the alternative."

"No! No! No! No!" This is the most Sheldon has said since I entered the room.

"Continue reading without stopping." Vince picks his packet back up as Sheldon continues.

"Based on nineteen specific criteria, I was selected for my particular assignment. I will be fully trained and equipped to complete my assignment. I will be given all of the necessary resources in order to comply with The Agency directives."

"Thank you. Next."

The next inductee begins reading. He is an older man. Probably in his seventies. I'm surprised he hasn't had a heart attack based on the information we've been told thus far. "I must never reveal the directives or operations of The Agency. If at any point, I reveal to a non-agency individual any of the information shared by The Agency, my assignment will be terminated and I will be sent immediately to Hell."

"Thank you. The last paragraph please." Vince motions toward the sole female inductee in the room.

She clears her throat before she begins. As she opens her mouth to speak, tears fall from her eyes. "Our organization is comprised of members from all facets of life. In the political arena, there are state government departments and agencies run by members of The Agency. There are local government officials as well as community organization leaders. There are courts and tribunals that Agency staff have full control over. There are members of The Agency in sports, law enforcement, television and radio broadcasting, global media technology, and space exploration. Our two largest industries are music and religion. In music, we have members in every genre. In religion, we have leadership in each of the 4,186 religions on Earth represented by the 12 major categories: Baha'i, Buddhism, Christianity, Confucianism, Hinduism, Islam, Jainism, Judaism, Shinto, Sikhism, Taoism, and Zoroastrianism."

"Thank you." Vince says. His back is to me as he faced the woman reading who is seated directly across from me at the circular table. "Don't turn to page 2 yet. At this point, we're going to take a short break. There are restrooms down the hall to the left. If you go to the restroom, you will be accompanied by your security detail. If you choose to stay in the room, you can ask your Chief Presenter any questions you like at this point. Be back and ready to proceed in 10 minutes."

Nobody moves. Each of the inductees is staring at Vince like we're looking at a ghost. Technically, we are. I believe everyone is in a state of shock and doesn't know what to do. Who dare be the first person to move or speak?

Alexander taps me on the shoulder which seems to pull me out of a trance. I had honestly forgotten he was seated next to me. "Do you need a restroom break?" he asks.

"Uh... no." I don't know what else to say.

I notice that each of the Chief Presenters did exactly what Alexander just did. They woke their inductee of the trance by asking the same question. The older gentleman must have answered in the affirmative because he is standing up. I also see one of the security guards in the back of the room stand up. I assume he is the guard assigned to this elderly gentleman and is now going to take him to the restroom.

I turn back toward Alexander. I whisper as I'm too embarrassed to hear or say what I'm thinking. "I don't know how much more of this I can take... religion too? There are people who work for The Agency in religion?"

"Are you familiar with Bishop Harry Mel Clarksdale?" Alexander asks.

"Bishop H.M. Clarksdale?" Of course I'm familiar. Who hasn't heard of Bishop H.M. Clarksdale?" Bishop H.M. Clarksdale is probably the most popular preacher in the country. He has a tremendous following each week. He's on the internet, radio, television, and in movies. He's written a ton of books and his church has to seat at least 10,000 people. His services are standing room only every week. "Of course I heard of H.M. Clarksdale! Why? Does he work for The Agency too?"

"Yes." Alexander says. "He's on assignment."

"My mouth drops open. Literally. "What!" Everyone

who remained in the room looks at me. My statement wasn't as loud in my head as it was when it came out of my mouth. I remain focused on Alexander but I lower my voice significantly as I continue. "Bishop H.M. Clarksdale is on assignment? How? What's his assignment?"

"I'll tell you all about it later. It would take me more than 10 minutes to explain it to the point where you'd understand."

My mouth is still wide open. I'm totally shocked. As unbelievable as this entire situation is, this news is equally as shocking. I've personally never been a fan of Bishop Clarksdale but I certainly know who he is. I would think that every person in America, whether you're religious or not, has heard of him. Some people love him, some people hate him. Everyone has heard of him. How in the world is a pastor of that magnitude on an assignment as devious as this?

I hear the beep of the door opening and the older inductee reenters the room with his security guard. It's so difficult to fathom a man of his age on assignment. In one thought, I question how many more years he has to live because he's already an old man. In the very next thought, I'm reminded that he died already so I guess it doesn't matter. In the next thought, I question what kind of assignment would an inductee like he have. He certainly couldn't be a security guard. In the next thought, I think about some of the people I saw downstairs at the registration tables. Most of them were older people. I didn't take notice to it then and hadn't considered the fact that each of them is probably on assignment. Maybe their sole responsibility in all this is to register inductees for training.

I look at Vince to see if the orientation is ready to continue. He's in a private conversation with one of the security guards. He has a bottle of water in his hand and is still holding his packet in the other. He and the guard share a private joke of sorts because both laugh as the guard returns to his seat. Vince turns and looks at each of us seated next to our Chief Presenter. He places his water bottle on the table as he continues. "Okay let's get back into it. Everyone turn to page 2 in your orientation packet. I'm going to read this to you myself. I'm not here to insult your intelligence to suggest that you can't read it on your own. However, it is standard procedure for me to read this to you. This part of the orientation may answer questions you have as to who we are as an organization. So if you will simply follow along as I read The History of The Agency."

The History of The Agency

In the world before creation, the spirits existed solely and for their own purpose. Each to his own cause and led by a visionary few. With any collection of visionary thoughts, counter thoughts and ideas began to clash and a disagreement ensued. With no resolution amongst the council of the visionary spirits, a separation that ultimately resulted in warfare erupted. The result of warfare is the creation of the Earth and mankind. The spoil of war are the souls loved by the visionary creative spirits. The visionary spirits have been at battle over the souls of mankind since the beginning of the physical creation.

The Agency dates back to the conflict between the Egyptians and the Caananites won by Pharaoh Thutmose III. It was after this conflict that recorded history began to be taken and The Agency began. The Agency was originally unnamed yet it was referred to as The Resistance. The Resistance was founded by visionary spirits who initiated the concept with 12 colonies. These colonies initiated a widespread campaign to engage in conflict for the capturing of souls and the growing of The Resistance. Within the first 30 years, The Resistance grew to over 37 million individuals.

The formal name of The Agency came centuries later. The warfare became more elaborate as technology advanced and as civilizations took more modernized form. Today, The Agency employs more than 2 billion people on any one given day. Every individual associated with The Agency is living in the afterlife.

Behind every human conflict is the conflict of the spirit

world. Members of The Agency have held positions of executive leadership in the Earth for centuries and are masterminds at the human conflict. The Agency is the world's largest organized entity. The Agency has offices in every major city on Earth and monitors the assignments of over 3 billion individuals. Every day the organization grows as there are people who transition from life to death daily. Every day the organization loses members as individuals choose to not complete their assignment.

The Agency thrives on the extreme intellect of visionary spirits and carefully selected member positions. Individuals are selected based on their beforelife careers and expertise. Successful industry leaders before death have attained equal success after death in the same or similar industry. Using this line of thought, The Agency has been able to grow and maintain its position as the only opposition between spirits.

The General Counsel of The Agency

The Agency is governed by an elected set of individuals called the general counsel. The assignment of each of these individuals is to leverage their expertise of judicial matters to formulate documentation for members of the afterlife on Earth. Any member of The Agency can present a bill to the general counsel for consideration. In order for a bill to become Agency law it would have to be approved by a majority of the general counsel. A bill is enacted into Agency law by a process only known to three departments of the general counsel. These departments are H. E. (Human Endeavors), P&MM (Property and Material Matters), and F.S. (Financial Services). All Agency laws and codes come from one, two or all three of these departments that make up the general counsel. Agency members who are members of the general counsel do not have to necessarily be members of a particular department, group or committee.

The Membership of The Agency

All Agency members are known as Operatives. Each Operative is on a particular assignment. No single assignment is ever managed by one Operative. Each Operative working as primary position in a given assignment has the assistance of a Secondary Operative, a Resource Operative, a Guidance Operative and Assistant Operatives. Operatives are placed in training courses immediately as they enter the afterlife. Operatives are given their particular assignment upon successful completion of The Agency training courses.

All Operatives abide by a code of conduct which strictly encourages discretion and secrecy. Any Operative who informs a beforelife non-member of the existence of The Agency or their assignment will be immediately removed from The Agency and sent to their final demise.

"Your Chief Presenter will go into more detail and answer the variety of questions you have regarding The Agency and how you play a significant role in what we're here to do." Vince continues. "Please turn to the next page in your orientation packet."

Each of the inductees in the room turns to the next page in the packet. I quickly glance over it and pay attention to the title at the top of the page. The Assignment.

"The next section is very important for you to pay attention to. It is regarding the assignment. This is the most important reason you and each of us are here so pay close attention." Vince looks at the page and begins to read. "Every agency member in the afterlife on Earth is on an assignment. Every Operative on the Earth is either actively working an assignment or in training to receive an assignment. The assignment is the most important aspect to your afterlife existence. The assignment is the greatest development of the creative and visionary founders of The Agency. Without assignments, each Operative would already live their final existence in Hell. Instead, each Operative has the opportunity to prolong their final destination."

Vince pauses and looks up from his manual. He addresses us in a serious tone. "I want to pause right here to make something clear. There is a popular and common expression that many people say often; the lesser of two evils. People living in the beforelife have no idea how much truth is in that simple expression. What you're going through now is absolutely the embodiment of that expression; the lesser of two evils. As horrendous as your situation seems to you now, not participating in this training process or your assignment leads to a much worse fate."

Vince places his manual down on the circular desk. He leans against the desk without sitting on it and folds his arms. "This is the part of the training where I usually get personal. As I said in the intro, I have been on assignment for 31 years. My assignment is training. I introduce new Operatives such as yourselves to The Agency and do my best to describe what The Agency is. The thing about working an assignment, for me at least, is two things. What your focus is and how you put your energy into it. I teach people to allow your assignment to refocus your thoughts. Allow it to distract you. You will get full training on the power of distraction as one of your courses. Just in terms of explanation, you want to divert your thoughts as to not focus on your ultimate end. If you focus on the end, it will cause your current existence to be miserable. The more you can learn to divert your attention, the better you will ultimately..."

"But I don't understand! How can you focus on anything else? This is terrible! I can't believe this is happening to me! What did I do to deserve this! Huh? What did I do?" The female screams out through tears of anguish. "There's no way out of this? I'm sorry! I'm sorry for whatever I did! I'm sorry!"

As her personal security guard begins to stand, Vince signals him to remain seated. "Suzanne," he says "the rules have been explained by your Chief Presenter. You can either work for us or go back now. Your choice. This is the last time this will be explained. Make a decision now."

We learn her name for the first time. Suzanne. She looks to be in her mid-thirties. Although her cries and frustrating outburst were seemingly uncontrollable, Vince's words proved to be stronger. The lesser of two evils indeed. When faced with the possibility of going back, any sane person would comply. Vince has a calm demeanor but his words are direct. He doesn't raise his voice. He doesn't have to. The impact of our new reality is more powerful than any tone, octave, pitch or volume that his voice could obtain. Suzanne, like any of us would, calms down instantly. Her tears continue and her breathing is still heavy but the outburst is finished. Her Chief Presenter places a hand on her back to calm her and slow her breathing. Suzanne looked as if she would hyperventilate and pass out. She doesn't say another word. Vince has gained control of the room and continues without addressing her again.

"I'm going to go over a list of your training courses after we break for lunch. You'll notice within that list that there are trauma classes that you can take in our Emotion Recovery Building. Emotional Recovery is set up to help inductees cope with this situation. Anyone working with you on your transition team, myself as your lead trainer, your Chief Presenter, your security, etc. can end your assignment and send you back. We however, wish to work with you to prevent you going to your final anguish too early. There are trained counselors who specifically dealt with grief counseling before becoming members of The Agency. Their sole assignment is to assist inductees who are trying to make the mental transition. Based on the Chief Presenter that you have working with you, you may be able to attend the grief training instead of being sent back. If you show potential in being able to accept and complete your assignment, the Chief Presenter may request you be strengthened instead of discarded. In such event, you will attend Emotional Recovery or ER."

I sit quietly in shock. I can't believe these people are so organized. I can't believe everyone in this room is so calm. The inductees, including myself, have a look of controlled horror which is understandable. Everyone else however looks as if this is business as usual, although we all share the same fate. From what I gather from Alexander, this could all end in any moment. Unlike Vince who has been on Earth for many years working with The Agency, my time with The Agency could literally be a few hours. If this all could end as quickly as I have been told, how can anyone function normally? The fear of going back to Hell is absolutely a motivating tool to stay in line but at some point, I would think one would succumb to the thought of this predicament.

"As I was saying, this is what you make of it. Your choice. There is absolutely remorse and regret that come with this. At the same time, there's much work to be done. I can look at this as thirty years of a death sentence or thirty years of a life sentence. The choice I make determines what type of day I will have. I don't want to be miserable so I don't focus on miserable things." Vince takes a sip of water before he calmly continues. "One of the interesting things about The Agency is that we monitor individuals closely. We understand many of our new members more than they understand themselves. In other words, let me use myself as an example. I'm a trainer for The Agency. My assignment is to teach you all the basics about The Agency and this new life you now have. The reason I was given this assignment is because I was an executive trainer before I was killed. I taught leadership seminars and management for the

United States Air Force. Since my purpose from birth has been to teach, it was natural for me to be assigned this position. Here I am, thirty years later." Vince steps away from the desk in which he was leaning and begins to walk inside of the circle. "You may be assigned something based on your prior occupation like I was. You may be assigned something totally opposite of your occupation or career. So how is your assignment determined? Your assignment lies within your purpose. In my beforelife, I happened to discover my purpose and worked in it. That's why I was so happy doing what I did. It was my purpose. Now in death, I work in my purpose. This comes like second nature to me. If you happened to recognize your purpose and turn it into a career, then you will be assigned something very similar. If you never came into your purpose but died, you will be assigned something in line with your purpose and may need some training in order to perform your purpose. In either case, The Agency is very well versed on who you are. We have been studying each of you for many years. Like I said, we know you better than you know yourself."

I turn to Alexander with a bewildered look on my face. The more I learn of The Agency, the more astonished I am. Who has the time to do all of this? How? How do they find out what a person's purpose is if that person doesn't even find out? Alexander looks back at me without smiling or any real expression. He simply looks back at me, then back to Vince. This tells me that I need to continue to pay attention.

"A significant part of your training and development in The Agency is understanding human thoughts and emotions. We're going to teach you the human mind. This will help you in whatever assignment you're given. You'll then see how important a person's purpose is in doing what we do and how we understand more about a person than they do." Vince answered my question without me having asked. I have three billion more questions to ask but I dare not raise my hand. I sit and try to contain the fact that I want to run away screaming from this room, these people and this situation.

A loud buzzing sound comes through a speaker close to the ceiling in the room. Every new inductee in the room jumps a little from being startled. Suzanne holds her hand on her chest as to try to calm her nerves.

"That sound is a five minute alarm. We have five minutes to end this segment of your training and move to the next thing which is a tour and explanation of our facility here. I use the final few minutes before the tour to answer any questions you may have at this point. I know there are a lot of questions going through your mind. Let me assure you that you can be comfortable asking me anything at this juncture. After that, we'll start the tour."

The silence in the room can be cut with a knife. I don't think anyone has the guts to say anything. I glance out of the corner of my eye at the other three inductees. Each is looking at Vince like he is a ghost. No one says anything. No one moves.

"No one ever is bold enough to ask the first question. This happens with every class I train. So I'll ask and answer the question that is on your mind the strongest. Is there any way you can get out of this situation? The answer to that question is no. There is no way out. You either go back now or go back later. No one knows when that later is. So it would behoove you to delay that for as long as you can.

Another popular question is what you did to deserve your new reality. I can't answer that because each person has a different set of reasons. Your Chief Presenter can review your case file with you and you can get the answer to that question then."

"I've had dreams of... that place, ever since yesterday. I can't sleep. Will that ever stop?" Suzanne asks. She is still wiping tears from her eyes.

"Yes, that will stop. Each of you has had one dream so far. That's done on purpose and you'll learn more about that later. But in a nutshell, we have the ability to influence your dreams. So we give you a forty five second reminder of what Hell is. It helps with the overall mission of The Agency's compliance record." Vince responds.

"What is a compliance record?" I ask.

"Good question." Vince says. "Without going into too much detail because you're gonna learn about this later, compliance means the success rate from transitioning individuals from their beforelife reality to their afterlife reality. So for example, right now, there are four of you here. If after our training, two of you don't make it because you can't handle it, then I will have a fifty percent success rate for this particular class. The Chief Presenters of the two individuals who don't make it will have a negative score and could be penalized based on how many negative scores they receive. By invading your dreams and reminding you how bad it is to go back, our rate of keeping people working for The Agency is substantially higher. We all benefit that way. I benefit as your trainer if all four of you make it through the training and receive your assignment. Your Chief

Presenter benefits. Even the security detail assigned to you benefits. If you, for whatever reason, fail to at least take your assignment, it's potentially bad for all of us."

"If I mess this up, it's bad for you?" I quickly turn to Alexander and whisper my question to him.

"Yes." He whispers back. "We'll talk about it later."

"Are there any more questi..."

Another buzzer sound comes through the loud speaker.

"Never mind." Vince says. "It's our time slot to start our tour. Everyone get up and leave your packets here."

"Alright, let's go." Alexander says as he stands up. Everyone in the room stands. Vince walks from inside the circular table and approaches the door. He opens the door. Each of the inductees and Chief Presenters follow. The security guards remain in the room.

As I enter the hall, I see other people coming out of rooms on this floor. I quickly ascertain that there are two other inductee trainings similar to mine taking place. It seems as if we are all taking a tour of the building at the same time as each room lets out its new inductees, Chief Presenters and Trainers. From a quick glance, I can already tell who the other inductees are. Each of us undoubtedly feel the exact same way about this situation, this day, this training and this tour. We would give anything in the world to go back 24 hours and do something different as to not be where we are now.

Vince turns around to address my group, four new

inductees with four Chief Presenters. "There are three groups taking the tour but I'll be doing the talking for our group. Each group has their own trainer who will be doing the same thing I'm doing. Talking his or her group through the various aspects of the facility here. So, let's get started. This floor that we're on now, the fifteenth floor is for training. Floors thirteen through seventeen are set up just like this one. The rooms are identical and every day, a new set of inductees is ushered in."

We're walking down the hall and we pass the elevators. We pass the other classrooms where the two training classes are being held. Each of the three groups of people are walking toward the end of the hall with the other two classes ahead of ours.

Vince continues. "The only other room on this floor not used for training is the media control center. I'm gonna show you that room now. The media control center is a room that links audio and video feeds into every training room on the floor. Each floor has its own center. This center is linked to the three classrooms on this floor. The one downstairs is linked to the three classrooms on the fourteenth floor and so on."

The first training class gets to the media control center first. As their trainer, an older African American man, opens the door, his trainees and Chief Presenters go inside. The door closes. We are left standing in the hall with the other group. Although both groups have now stopped walking and are seemingly waiting for their turn to enter the media control center, neither group intermingles with the other. We all stand in silence as each of our respective trainers continues talking.

"Each of you will report to this floor as this is your assigned floor for the next four weeks. Your Chief Presenters will be with you each day and will ensure that you're all present, accounted for, and on time. The only time you will leave this floor during the next four weeks is for lunch. The cafeteria is on the second floor and we'll go there each day together. Other than that, this is your new home away from home. As I mentioned, food is located on the second floor. They serve breakfast, lunch and dinner and are fully staffed with some of the best chefs to ever live in the beforelife. You're more than welcome to come early for breakfast but make sure you're in our room and in your chair by 9:00 am. Period. Sharp. Don't ever be late."

The door to the media control room opens. I expect to see the first group come out so that the second group can go in. Instead, the second room steps into the room after their trainer. The door closes. The nine of us, four new inductees, four Chief Presenters, and Vince our trainer now stand in the hall and await our time to enter the room.

"We'll be going in in about two minutes. Do you guys have any questions before we go in?" Vince asks.

"So... the people who are there now..." Sheldon's voice is trembling. He, like the rest of us is having a very difficult time with this news.

"Where now? In Hell?" Vince interrupts and asks directly.

"Yeah... so they couldn't handle... working for The Agency?"

"Not necessarily. Only specific people were selected by

The Agency to work for us. The selections are based on your beforelife and how you conducted yourself then. We look at Agency needs and fill our needs based on humans in the beforelife. If we select someone who doesn't perform their assignment or cannot handle the pressure, they go back and are in Hell now regretting it. If a person was not selected by The Agency and dies, then that person goes to Hell based on how they lived in their beforelife. That person goes immediately and can't return. So that's who is there now. Those who were never chosen by The Agency in the first place and those who were selected but did not complete their assignment."

When I think about the horror of that place, it rocks me to my core. I feel like I'm going to pass out and fall on the floor when I remember it. They say I only experienced a few seconds of it. I can't imagine being there forever. If anything would cause a person to do whatever is required of them, the thought of avoiding Hell is it. I'd become President, CEO and Chairman of the Board for The Agency to avoid Hell. Whatever they ask me to do, whatever my assignment is, I would do it to the best of my ability for as long as they allow me. I don't care what it is.

"Does The Agency have a president or board members?" I blurt out a question without thinking. I had no intent on asking a question. I obviously have no desire being on this tour of the facility. No one would. Yet the question popped into my head and the next thing I know, it came flying out of my mouth.

"Wow!" Vince smiles and looks at Alexander. "Now that's a question I don't hear often. Great question." The other Chief Presenters smile as if they are proud of

Alexander's mentee. These people lack of focus of reality is unbelievable. I honestly don't believe I'll ever laugh again given my current circumstance. Yet these guys are chuckling based on me asking a question that apparently is a good question. "There is an executive leadership branch. One of your classes covers all of the top positions so I won't go into detail right now. But suffice to say, this organization is well led and well organized. We have a board of directors, a board chair, what you would refer to as a president and a cabinet. There are regional managers, district officers, trainers, chief presenters, local managers, facility managers, executive security management, you name it."

The door to the media control center opens. Vince notices and holds the door open for us to begin to walk in. As I follow the others in my group into the media control center, I think back to my neighbor Lawrence. He spoke to Alexander as if he knew him. Alexander spoke back. Lawrence smiled at me as if he knew what I was going through in that moment.

"This is the media control center." Vince gets back on track with the tour as the last person in our group enters the room. Vince closes the door behind himself as he comes in last.

I glance around the room. There are computer monitors everywhere. The room is dark and only illuminated by the computers at the work stations. This room reminds me of the NASA space station rooms I would see in the movies. There would be people in front of individual computers and then a large screen at the front of the room. Just like in the movies, there are people seated and working. They seem unbothered by us. I also see the group of new inductees that just came in before we did. They are walking out of a door on the other side of the room. That explains why they didn't come out the same door that they walked in.

"This building has cameras in every room. The cameras are monitored by these members of The Agency. There are different angles and the cameras are always recording. Nothing gets past this team in terms of things that happen inside the facility. Every floor, every elevator, every stairwell, every room. As I stated earlier, floors thirteen through seventeen are identical training floors. Each has its own media control center. The center has two responsibilities. They monitor what happens on their own floor and they monitor what happens in certain areas of the building. This control center monitors the fifteenth floor because that is the floor that we are on. They can see every training class. If something were to go wrong, they would see it and be able to request backup security if needed. Each of you new folks are watched closely as you begin training. If you have an emotional outburst, these people see it in your face, your body language, or your responses. If the need arises to remove you from the training and the premises, they will know it even before a person like myself or your Chief Presenter. This is their assignment and they're very good at what they do."

As Vince is explaining, I'm looking at the people seated in front of the computer monitors. They look like robots. They are emotionless and expressionless. They are staring at their computer screens. Some are typing. Some are speaking softly into headsets. No one is paying attention to our class or Vince. Our tour seems routine to everyone except the four new inductees in my training class. We're utterly amazed at the organization and the horror of this.

They are all going forward as business as usual, just another day at work.

"Now if you'll all follow me..." Vince makes his way to the front of the group. He walks past the staff members working diligently at monitoring their computers and leads us to the door at the other side of the room. We all go through the second door. He allows us all to go in and then closes the door behind himself. "...this room is connected to our global control tower. Similar to the media control room, this room monitors activity within our city and state. I mentioned earlier in the training that every major city in the world has a branch headquarters. Through control towers, we monitor the movements of every person connected to The Agency. This is for accountability and security."

"But why? Why is it so important to watch everybody like this?" Suzanne blurts out in a frustrated tone. As I look at her and see the frustration on her face, I notice the older gentleman. He is standing next to her and weeping uncontrollably. I hadn't noticed him crying or saying much before but now I can literally hear him crying and feel the heavy breathing. He looks as if he is having a heart attack yet no one offers to help him. His Chief Presenter has his hand on his back and Vince proceeds to answer Suzanne's question as if the older gentleman isn't having a massive attack. I have yet to learn this man's name.

"If one of you decides that the pressure is too much for you and cannot fulfill your assignment, you will be sent back. If you decide to try to escape, we will find you... quickly. Through technology and the systems in this room, we can track the whereabouts of any member of The Agency at any given time. I'll give you a quick example."

Vince places his hand on the shoulder of one of the staff members in this control tower. He whispers into this person's ear and the person begins typing.

This room is very similar to the room we just left except there are larger monitors. The screens at the front of this room are larger than life. The images are constantly changing on the screens from street views, to aerial views, to inside other buildings. The images are rotating and changing.

"I just asked this staff member to find me. She should be able to locate me in a matter of second..."

"Found you." The lady says. She presses a button on her keyboard and the image on the huge screen is of us, standing in the room. There is a camera in the room pointed directly at Vince. Since Vince is standing with us, we can all now see ourselves on screen.

"The system was able to locate me by a tracking device that is a part of me. Within seconds, we can find any person who has had that device grafted into their body. This is how we keep track of all members. Does anyone remember how many members I said were part of The Agency?"

"A tracking device! What? Are you serious? A tracking device! This is too much!" I say. I feel like I'm next in line to have a heart attack. "We have to have a tracking device placed on us?" As loud as I am, no one from the control tower even glances in my direction. They continue the work whatever each of them is assigned to do.

"Remember when Alexander and... who was with you?" Vince directs his question from me to Alexander.

"Josh and Kevin." Alexander answers.

"Right." Vince turns back to me. "Remember when Alexander, Josh and Kevin placed something very hot on your leg to remind you what Hell felt like? Well that served as your mental reminder. It helps to keep people in line. If you get a five second feel of that, you're more apt to comply with whatever anyone is asking of you. At the same time, it's our way of inserting the tracking device. Each of you has already been branded if you will. One of the responsibilities of the Chief Presenter and security personnel is to brand the new inductees before they arrive for the first day of training. Then, as soon as you walk through the front door of the building, your body connects with the server. We now can follow you until you are disconnected from The Agency. This happens every day, all across the world and is monitored in rooms like this all across the globe."

I immediately grab my leg in a state of petrified shock! They've inserted a tracking device inside me! This experience becomes more horrifying with every new aspect that is explained to me! I'm brushing my leg furiously and I notice the other inductees doing the same. Suzanne is brushing her arm. The other two are also brushing their leg. For the first time, Suzanne's Chief Presenter, a female, speaks. "You can't brush it off. You can't remove it. If you were to try to run and escape, this is how you would be followed and apprehended."

"Will it hurt us? Is it in my blood stream? I have a weak heart!" The older gentleman cries out.

Vince responds. "You're already deceased. Your heart is fine now." Vince has become extremely blunt as the day has progressed. What he says makes sense. If we're already dead, you can't die of a heart attack. What he said however has sent shock waves through me. I honestly don't know how much more of this I can take. They are tracking my every movement and the movement of millions of people through computers and tracking devices.

This is the most disciplined organization I have ever seen and I never even knew it existed. This is equally as incredible as it is overwhelmingly terrible.

"We're on a tight schedule folks. We have another room to see before we break for lunch. Let's keep it moving." Vince brings order to the chaos that just erupted. At this point, everyone knows the consequence of non-compliance. Whatever despicable thing we learn next wouldn't be as horrendous as being sent back. They understand this well and have made sure we have a constant reminder if we ever consider not following Agency directives. No one in their right mind would choose to go back versus working for The Agency. For that reason, The Agency has billions of members.

We follow Vince out of this room through another door. This door is directly across the room from the door we entered to walk into the control tower. This seems like a hall of rooms with one room leading to the next room. As we enter the next room, I see cubicles. Each cubicle has a person working in it like an average office building. "These Agency members are responsible for the daily activities of this particular building. They are in charge of everything from building maintenance and upkeep, loading and unloading of equipment and freight, food and catering services, IT and technical support, landscaping of the surrounding grounds, building security, and scheduling. So if the parking lot needed to be repaved, for example, someone in this room would be responsible for doing all that would have to be done to get that taken care of. If the computer systems aren't working properly, they fix it in a hurry. They keep the cafeteria downstairs set up with food for our breakfast and lunch breaks. Those are the kinds of things this team handles. You guys have any questions?"

"I have a question." I say. "So... a person's assignment is based on what they did in their professional life before they died right? So all of these people did similar work prior to them dying?"

"That's the case in most people's situations but it depends. It's not so much what you did for a living but what your purpose was." Vince walks to one of the staff workers sitting at a cubicle. A middle age White man. "Excuse me, can I ask you something?" Vince says to the man.

"Sure." The young man turns in his chair towards us.

"Can you give my new trainees your personal story of your beforelife experience and why this is your assignment?"

"Not a problem. Hey everybody my name is Patrick and this is my fourth year with The Agency. In my beforelife, I was a government employee. I was employed with the Department of Transportation. With The Agency, I manage all incoming and outgoing shipments, packages and vehicles. If we are in need of..." he takes a moment to think of an example, "...toilet tissue. An order is placed and that has to be shipped here. Once it arrives at the loading dock, it has to be checked in and signed for. The package then has to be taken to housekeeping and etcetera etcetera. So I manage operations such as this. Whether its bathroom supplies, new computer equipment, air condition and heating parts, or if the water cooler isn't working. I handle all the transporting and incoming and outgoing of all of that. Everything is closely monitored. If that toilet paper doesn't arrive in the proper bathroom, I will see it in a report somewhere. Then we have to fix it. Diligently."

"Thanks for the explanation." Vince says as he shakes Patrick's hand.

"Not a problem." Patrick turns back around in his chair and picks up his desk phone. He begins to dial as we walk away.

"So as you can see, we are a very fit organization." Vince says as he begins to walk the group toward yet another door. "The Agency has been around for centuries. Through the genius of those who have created and built our infrastructure, you can believe that no stone has been unturned. They have thought of everything, considered everything and analyzed everything.

Vince walks to the other side of the room and opens the door. As the group follows, I can't help but to glance at each person seated at a desk. Each of these individuals is dead, yet alive. Each has a story as Patrick does. Each has had an experience like I had. Each has been through training and accepted this lot as the greatest lesser of two evils ever conjured. I would be interested in hearing each of their stories like I just heard Patrick's. How do they handle it? How are they so composed? Do they actually come in here every single day of the week like this is a regular job and that everything is just okay? How do you sleep at night? How am I going to sleep tonight?

Walking through this door leads us back into the hallway. Vince turns around and faces us as soon as we are all out of the room. "Okay guys. That ends the tour of this floor and for the most part, our morning session. We break for lunch and our dining facility is downstairs on the like I mentioned. You're going to go down with your Chief Presenters for lunch. As they will probably tell you, our dining facility is top notch in all of our locations so feel free to eat as much or as little as you want. Your Chief Presenter will probably tell you this but I will say it first." Vince presses the button on the elevator to go down. "Eat something. Eat a lot. I know that what you're experiencing is a lot to take in. As a matter of fact, we know exactly how your brain is processing the information I'm giving you. You need to eat though. You have to. As difficult as this is, your body needs it." The elevator opens and Vince holds it open for us to get on. "Enjoy your lunch and I'll see you guys back in the training room in an hour."

The last time I saw a dining facility this elaborate was on a business trip where my colleagues and I were treated to lunch at the Four Seasons. This restaurant however is nicer than that one. The entire floor is the restaurant. The restaurant has glass doors right across from where the elevator opens. The room can easily hold four hundred people at a time. It seems to be just that crowded. I assume everyone in the building is at lunch at the same time. I look at the other inductees and they look like tourists on their first visit to Times Square in New York City. We're looking around in amazement at the sheer elegance of what I thought would be a lunchroom cafeteria. The windows are from floor to ceiling and the view is of all of downtown. The drapery and linen are top notch. There are probably fifteen huge chandeliers hanging from the ceiling. The food is buffet style. I see a huge meat carving station, a shrimp and lobster station, every kind of fruit one can imagine, pastas, pastries, you name it. "This is the lunch room?"

"Nice isn't it?" Alexander answers.

"Nice? This is beautiful! What in the world? Why all this for a lunch room?"

"I'll explain once we sit down to eat. What kind of food do you like?"

"Um, I have no idea. This is overwhelming." I once again glance around the room while talking to Alexander and I can't believe the level of this décor or the type of food being served. The servers are wearing chef hats and aprons. There are men and women walking around wearing tuxedos catering to people as they sit and eat. This is unbelievable.

"What do you suggest? Everything looks... incredible!"

"Let's get Chinese." Alexander says as he points toward the left side of the room.

"Okay that's fine." Chicken, beef, pork, stir fry, egg rolls, soup. They have it all. Alexander chooses a table that four men are already seated at. There are two open chairs and he politely asks if the two chairs are open. One man motions for us to have a seat.

I quickly determine that one of the four men is sitting alone. The other three know each other and are talking. I want to ask them how long they have been with The Agency. I want to ask how they are handling it. I want to find out what their assignments are. I have so many questions upon questions that I wish to know. I dare not say a word. I don't know if those kinds of questions are allowed, encouraged or discouraged.

"I'm Alexander, Chief Presenter. This is Brian, new inductee." Alexander introduces us. I didn't remember that my name is now Brian. The three men that seemingly know each other look up. The fourth man continues to eat with his face looking down, directly into his plate of food. It's as if he didn't hear Alexander say a word.

"Hey man, I'm Wil."

"Sylvester."

"Clarence."

"This your first day here?" Sylvester asks me.

The fourth man immediately grabs his plate of food, utensils and glass and gets up from the table. He walks away without having introduced himself nor saying a word. I watch the man walk away. He chooses to sit at a table where no one else is currently sitting. He puts his plate down with his glass and utensils. As he sits, he looks back toward us. We look at one another before he turns and looks down at his plate again.

I now wonder what is going through his mind and heart. I can only imagine the turmoil he is dealing with which has caused him to be so antisocial. I understand this man even without speaking with him. I feel the pain he must feel. Amidst the outstanding décor and exquisite cuisine, the fact remains that everyone in this room is going to Hell. How anyone can eat and converse and laugh and live is hard to fathom... except for the other option.

I look back at Sylvester who is awaiting my answer as if the fourth gentleman didn't just abruptly walk away. I open my mouth to respond but I don't hear my own voice. Nothing comes out of my mouth.

"Yeah, first day." Alexander answers for me.

"Yeah, you can always tell the newbies. Still in a state of shock. Don't worry, you'll grow into this and be okay. All you gotta do is fall in love with your time."

"Uh, yeah. Thanks." My voice finally works. I taste the food. This is the best Chinese food I've ever had. "How long have you been here?"

"With The Agency... I been here for seven years, three months, twenty six days. I'm in love with my time. I cherish every moment I have so I'm aware of every second." he responds.

"This is my second year with The Agency." Wil answers without being asked directly.

"I've been here the longest of the three of us. Eleven years." Clarence says.

I turn to Alexander who is eating. "I never asked you how long you've been with The Agency."

"I've been with The Agency for six years." Alexander says.

Six years for Alexander. Eleven years for Clarence. Thirty years for Vince. These are prison sentences. Yet, the other option is worse. I can't imagine spending eleven years or even eleven days in Hell. That will be my reality though... someday.

"Is it appropriate if I ask a question?" I direct my question toward Alexander who is sitting next to me.

"Yeah. If your question isn't appropriate, I'll let you know."

"I'm just curious to know you guys' role with The Agency now. Like, what do you do and how do you cope?"

The guys look at one another to decide who answers first.

"I'm an attorney so I litigate cases. That's what I did in my former life. There are a lot of cases in my office that need to go a certain client's way if you will. I do my best to make sure The Agency interests are covered. I only stopped in here for lunch because the food is so good. My office is about four blocks from here." Sylvester says.

"So you make sure good people lose and go to jail or something?" I ask.

"Okay that's enough." Alexander places his hand on my arm to stop me from asking questions. I assume this question is digging too deep.

"No, it's okay. I'll answer that."

"Okay that's fine but we need to get ready to go back upstairs anyway. I want to get back early before the next session. We gotta finish eating and then head up."

"No problem. To answer your question, there are certain situations where The Agency may dictate how they want a certain person prosecuted. I have a lot of cases for example where a pastor is charged with financial or sexual misconduct. In some cases, we try to lock that person up. This may be to separate them from the people they are supposed to be leading. In other cases, we realize that he or she would become more powerful if locked up. So we try to instead make him or her a distraction to the followers. In any regard, we do a lot of research on the people who come into our office and see what The Agency needs are. That's what I do. How do I cope? I'm a very busy man. I don't think on it. I think about my job. I'm good at what I do. That's all."

I'm utterly amazed. I can't believe so much thought goes into this. I don't know how to respond to that, so I don't. Alexander and I finish eating without too much banter after that. I did learn that Clarence is also a trainer. He is in a similar role as Vince. Wil is an instructor. He specifically teaches one thing as opposed to Clarence and Vince who train all new inductees on the new life they now live. Once the new life phase of training is over, a person like Wil begins to work on someone's specific assignment.

Alexander and I are the first ones back to the room for training. Josh and Kevin met us at the elevator to go back. The four of us enter the room. Josh and Kevin take a seat on the side of the room where the security detail was seated earlier. Alexander and I sit down in the seats we were in for training.

"I have to be honest with you. I'm shocked that so much detail goes into this. What's so important about this Agency that all this research and dedication and commitment is put in?" I ask.

"As you learn more, that question will be answered. It's a good question. It would take me all week to try and answer. For now, just know that there is good and evil in the world and they battle against one another. This has been going on since before time even started. We're now caught up in that battle and have become a part of it."

"On the evil side?"

Just as I ask Alexander the question, the door opens. I'm not sure if everyone else in my training group ate lunch together but they enter the room together. Vince quickly takes control of the room as he is ready to get started.

"Okay everyone, if you'll take your seats we can continue. I trust everyone enjoyed their lunch." Vince opens with a statement more than a question.

I look at each of my fellow inductees. Maybe the lunch thing worked. Everyone looks more relaxed than when they left. Each person looks a lot less stressed out. These Agency folks really have this thing figured.

"Moving on, I'm going to talk about what the next training sessions will be for you and what you can expect." Vince says. "There are general classes that you have coming up. Those are... Human Emotion and Reason, Motivational Decision Making, The Fall of Life and The Fall of Man, and Assignments. You will have to pass each of these courses to graduate from the training and be granted your particular assignment. You don't have a choice in the matter. You have to take each class. You have to attend each class. You have to pass each class. No excuses. If you do not attend any particular session or if you do not pass the course in general, your assignment with The Agency will be terminated immediately and you will be sent back to Hell. Once again, if you are sent back to Hell, there is no coming back. You will be there forever. The only opportunity you have to avoid that dreaded place is to work your assignment with all that you have in you. Embrace it and work it. Eat it, sleep it, live it. Don't shorten your time."

I glance at each of my classmates. Suzanne, Sheldon and the older gentleman who I have yet to learn his name. I believe the reality is setting in on us again. Lunch was one of the finest cuisines I have ever had even though I've eaten in fine establishments over the course of my adult life. This however, was top notch. Even with that, the reality causes one to lose their composure. The older gentleman is seemingly having a difficult time again. He has his hand on his chest and seems to be having an attack. The only reason I, nor anyone else seems to panic is because of what Vince said earlier. You can't die from a heart attack if you're already dead. Vince moves on with what he is saying, despite how this gentleman is responding.

"Your classes begin tomorrow. What you're going to begin to learn in your classes is the way The Agency trains you to think and how different that thought process is from what you had been used to. For example, if you're being selected in an interactive position, you will be directly interacting with another person who has not died. Everything you do will be centered around getting that person to think a certain way. The end result will be how you get that person to think, react and respond. If you're being selected in a support position, you may work here in this facility or in another facility that we have in this district. You may support in a variety of ways. My job is support. One of you may be a trainer like I am. You may be selected as security or as Chief Presenter. All of those areas fall under support."

The older gentleman is crying and his Chief Presenter looks very concerned. I understand what Alexander said regarding having a heart attack after death but something seems to be wrong.

"I'll be right back." I turn toward Alexander as he whispers that into my ear. He stands up and walks out of the room.

Vince continues to speak as if none of this is going on. "There are rare occasions where new inductees are selected for leadership positions in The Agency. That however requires a different clearance and level of training. You'll learn about all the positions in The Agency when you go through The Rise and Fall class."

Sheldon raises his hand to ask a question. I wasn't aware that we could ask questions. Maybe his Chief Presenter made him aware that he could ask.

"Yes?" Vince acknowledges Sheldon.

"Um, what happens if you're given an assignment that you don't want or that doesn't suit you?"

"Good question." Vince says. "The assignment you're given is based on your specific case study. As we speak, there is a team of people who are studying each of you. We are determining your purpose and why you were created in the first place. Based on a set of equations, we're able to study you both before and after you die. So the assignment you're given is based on what you're purpose is and what you're gifted to do. You can choose to not accept or fulfill your assignment but that terminates your membership in The Agency and sends you to Hell immediately."

As Vince makes this statement, the old man cries out. "Oh no! God please help me! Save me Jesus! Please!"

"Frank! Calm down! Calm down!" I just learned the older man's name is Frank as his Chief Presenter tries to calm him. He is patting him on the back and calling his name. "Take it easy!"

The door opens and Alexander rushes back in. He has water and what looks like a breathing apparatus. "Drink this, it will calm you." Alexander gives Frank the glass of water. The man is shaking so hard that it's difficult for him to drink it. He does drink however and hands Alexander the glass when he is done. Alexander and Frank's Chief Presenter put the breathing thing over Frank's mouth. They make him put his head back and breathe. Everyone is looking at Frank and waiting to see what will happen next.

"Guys, let's escort Frank next door so he can calm down a little. Bring him back when he's ready." Vince says.

Frank's two security guards get up as well as his Chief Presenter. They help Frank out of his seat and walk him out the door. He is slowly walking while holding the breathing thing over his nose and mouth. It looks like it could be an oxygen mask but I don't see an oxygen tank. Once they are out of the room, Vince continues.

"Just so the rest of you know, we understand, here at The Agency, that what we're telling you and explaining is a lot to deal with. Especially on this your first day. We've set up professional counseling centers to talk you through some of your anxiety. That's where Frank is being taken. Once he is able to calm down, his Chief Presenter will bring him back and he can rejoin the training. If any of you feel faint or that you may need medical attention, let your Chief Presenter know. Keep in mind what I mentioned to Frank though, no matter how badly your chest hurts, you cannot have a heart attack in the afterlife. What you're experiencing in that moment is anxiety and fear, not an attack. Nonetheless, let someone know immediately if you require assistance."

No one moves. No one says one word. I'm positive, Sheldon and Suzanne are as shocked as I am and don't want to say or do anything. Vince continues and breaks the deafening silence in the room.

"Sheldon have I answered your question?" Vince asks Sheldon. Sheldon doesn't respond. Instead, he's looking at Vince like a deer caught in headlights on a dark road. "Sheldon?"

"Uh yes. Yes. Thank you." Sheldon responds in a noticeably shaken voice.

"Good. You two have any questions? Brian? Suzanne?" Neither I nor Suzanne respond. "Okay. So as I was saying, the classes begin tomorrow. The classes are very thorough. You're going to learn a lot and your thoughts will be challenged. You've been taught a lot of things in your beforelife which will be debunked in the training classes. You'll see the world and the people in it in an entire new light. You'll also learn about assignments and the way they are handed out. You'll get real examples and meet some people who are working their assignments and have been for years. Once you successfully learn all that they have to teach you, you'll be given your personal assignment. Your Chief Presenter will be with you the entire time. You can ask your Chief Presenter whatever you want. If you happen to ask a question that your Chief Presenter isn't allowed to answer, they will let you know that. You will be picked up and dropped off at your place of residence every day. You will receive continental breakfast each morning once you arrive for class. Your lunch will be in the same facility you had lunch today. Your dinner will be ready for you when you arrive home in the evening. There is already a chef in your home cooking right now. By the time you arrive at your personal residence this evening, one of your favorite meals will be prepared for you. You and your Chief Presenter can then eat and talk before you need to get rest. You want to make sure you have rest so you can be prepared for classes tomorrow."

I look at Alexander who is fixated on Vince. I want to ask if someone is in my condo right now. Someone is in my kitchen right now. How do they know what one of my favorite meals is? I choose to not say anything and continue to listen to Vince.

"Another important thing to remember. This is difficult to accept or understand but it's extremely important to your success with The Agency for you to get this. Remember... you... are... dead. Each of you had a life ending circumstance that occurred yesterday. Since you are dead, there are family members, friends, coworkers, neighbors, classmates, fraternity or sorority brothers, organization members, or anyone else mourning your loss. As you sit here and listen to me, there are people planning your funeral right now."

Suzanne starts crying. I admittedly begin to choke up. Mom is probably crushed. My sister... oh my God! I hadn't even thought about my family or friends since my thoughts have been so preoccupied with Hell.

"If you happen to see someone you know, you cannot run up to them and try to communicate. They will not recognize you."

What?

"If you look into a mirror, you will see yourself as you know yourself. Anyone else looking at you though will see a different you. So if you see your uncle and run up and say 'Uncle Joe! Uncle Joe it's me! Sharon!' your uncle Joe will freak out. He just buried his niece Sharon. You look nor sound nothing like the niece that he remembers. Instead, you look and sound like Suzanne. You see Sharon in the mirror. He sees Suzanne when he sees you... and he'll think you're a lunatic. You have to remember this. We do our best to avoid contact with anyone you know. There are times where we mess up and confrontations happen. So, for your own good, don't forget this."

I remember Alexander mentioning to me about my family and friends not being able to recognize me. This is crazy.

"The final thing you need to know is that your training will take four months." Vince says.

"Four months?" I speak out before I realize that I am speaking out.

"Yes. four months. Like I said, you have a lot of deprogramming and programming and reprogramming to go through before you get your assignment. The weeks are going to fly by. You're going to wonder where the time went. The classes are seven days per week. You do not get weekends off. Your time to relax and filter all of your information will be in the early afternoon and evenings. That's the time you'll spend with your Chief Presenter at dinner."

Suzanne and her Chief Presenter are holding hands. Suzanne is using her other hand to wipe her eyes with a tissue that someone gave her. Sheldon is looking as distressed as I'm feeling. The nostalgia from lunch has completely worn off. Reality has set in. We're all doomed to the pain and horror of Hell. I've only spent a few moments there and the pain was unbearable. The torture was excruciating. The smell was horrendous. The creatures were terrifying. The people were screaming. The fire was beyond a heat that I had ever experienced. The lake was on fire. The ground was on fire. I was on fire. My face and my arms and my legs were all burning with the intense fire. The reality that we are all going back is setting in. The only thing keeping all of the people in this situation sane is the mere fact that we can all work for The Agency and hopefully be here for centuries.

"Well, that's the end of your orientation guys." Vince says. "Anyone have any final questions?" No one says a word. "The packet that you received when you first came in has just about everything I have said today word for word. If you have any questions on most of what I said, you can look through that booklet tonight. Your Chief Presenter will also be with you so you can ask questions if you need to." Vince leans against the circular table that he has been standing inside of all day today. He folds his arms and addresses in a calmer and less teacher tone. "Suzanne, Brian, Sheldon, this is the hardest thing you've ever had to deal with. Believe me when we say that we understand. Everyone in this room has sat in that same seat and cried or yelled or screamed. We've all been there. We simply realize that the best way to handle this is to prolong it by doing a good job. I really hope all of you make it through your four classes and graduate to your assignment. Do your assignment well... embrace your time... good luck!"

The entire ride from the training facility back to my condo was silent. I spent the ride looking out of the window and trying to process all that I learned today. I looked for familiar faces in the cars that sat in traffic around us. I tried to see if any of my coworkers would be walking to the subway. I saw a police officer and immediately wondered if he could help me. Then I thought he may be a member of The Agency. I thought about the thousands of times I've driven down the street where the training facility is located and never knew of its purpose. I thought about my dream when I saw Hell. I thought about Suzanne, Frank and Sheldon. I thought about Vince. I've replayed every moment of this horrendous day in my mind more than once. I would give every dollar I've ever owned to be rid of this existence.

Josh pulls over in front of a condominium that I'm not familiar with. Maybe this is where Kevin lives and he's being dropped off on the way to my place. Josh turns the vehicle off.

"This is your new residence." Alexander says to me. "You're in a condo on the second floor. Everything is already ready for you upstairs. I'll be staying with you tonight. Josh and Kevin will be down here."

"So... this is my new place? Why?" I ask.

"Can't go back to your old place. People are there. Your family. Your furniture eventually will be moved and the unit will be sold." Alexander replies. "We can never go back there."

"Oh. Okay. Makes sense."

There's an awkward silence where the four of us are simply sitting in the SUV.

"Alright let's go see your new place and have dinner." Alexander says as he opens his door.

"Wait... before we go up. Is it okay if I ask these guys a question?" I ask.

"Yeah. Go ahead."

"How did you guys... you know... die?" I ask.

Josh and Kevin look at one another to ascertain who will respond first.

"I was a bouncer in my beforelife. You know the club Vindictive City downtown?" Josh goes first.

"Yeah. I've been there." I say.

"Okay. I used to work there. Remember the shooting that made headlines because it was July 4th weekend? Killed four people?"

"Oh yeah, I remember that!"

"I was one of those four people. One night I was at work, the next thing I know, people are running around and falling over each other. A fight had broken out. Gunshots, I'm in the middle of it trying to get some type of order back, the next day I'm in The Agency building in orientation."

"Wow!" I remember that shooting. It made local news and shut Vindictive City down for a few months.

"My story is a little different." Kevin begins. "I met a woman who worked in the same department I worked in at my job. She was gorgeous. We would just smile at one another at first. One day, we bumped into one another in the hall. I introduced myself as did she. At the time, Hurricane Katrina had just devastated New Orleans and she mentioned it. Our conversation started there as we both had family in Louisiana. After that day, we started to purposely bump into one another. Then I asked her to lunch. She let me know that she was married which I already knew because she wore a ring. I told her that was fine and we met for lunch. That lunch date was the first of many dates over a two and a half year span. It started innocent and harmless but long story short, we fell in love. She was my soulmate and I was hers'. We went on trips together. We went to sporting events together. We just enjoyed each other. I was in love. We both were in love. Her husband suspected her of cheating and hired a private investigator. It didn't take long for the investigator to compile plenty of evidence against her and I. The next day, her husband came up to the job and waited in his car. When we got off work, he walked right up to me and pointed a gun at me. Boom! That was it! Next day, I'm at The Agency."

"Wow! Did he kill her too?" I ask.

"I don't know. My eyes closed and then one second later, my eyes opened in Hell. Since then, she's been the last thing on my mind."

I'm shocked by these stories. It is absolutely incredible what happened to Josh, Kevin and some of the others who have shared. As terrible as all of this is, it is fascinating at the same time. Alexander opens the door which indicates to me that it's time to get out and go to my new home.

"Welcome to your new home." Alexander hands me an envelope once we get to my door. I open it and slide a set of keys out of it. When I walk in and begin to look around, I see that they chose furniture and fixtures similar to what I already had. The place is very nice. My previous place was very nice. I would've picked this layout and design theme myself so I can tell they studied my previous place as they designed this place.

"It's nice. Real nice." I say.

"Reminds you of your old place?"

"Yeah."

"Good. The food is already ready. I'll get it. You make yourself comfortable but check out the paper on the table over there." Alexander walks into the kitchen. I still haven't moved. I look around once again. New... home. New... existence.

The paper on the table is a letter from The Agency. Brian, welcome to your new accommodations. We know you will find them to your liking. Please remember the following important bits of information. You are not allowed to leave the premises until you have graduated from the program. Your Chief Presenter Alexander will be available to answer any questions you have. You are to be downstairs every morning at 8:00 am. The letter is short and to the point.

Alexander walks from the kitchen with a steaming plate. Looks like steak and lobster. He has a bottle of wine and two glasses. "Dinner. Have a seat."

"Steak and lobster? When it comes to food, you guys really do it up huh?" I say as I sit at the table.

"It's definitely one of the perks." Alexander places my plate in front of me and walks back into the kitchen. He continues to talk to me from the kitchen. "They do a very good job at making life as enjoyable as they can because they recognize the other side of it. The main thing is to create an environment where you can focus on your assignment. That is so key and so important. At the end of the day, that's what all of this is about. Getting your assignment, being trained to perform it, doing it!" He walks from the kitchen with another plate for himself.

"So it's like this every night when I get home?" I ask.

"While you're in training, yes. Once training is over, things change a little. You'll be able to go out and shop for groceries, go to restaurants, whatever." Alexander says as he opens the bottle of wine. "It's definitely a perk for the Chief Presenter. We eat the best out of all the senior level support staff."

Just like lunch, the food is outstanding. The steak is cooked exactly how I like it.

"So I know you have a lot of questions you want to ask. Go head. Shoot." Alexander says as he eats.

"Okay. First of all I want to know how you guys know I like my steak cooked like this! How did you guys know what my favorite meal is? Or did they just assume because most people like steak and lobster?"

"The Agency is notorious for the level of research we do on individuals. How do they know you like lobster and steak? Well, while we were in orientation today, a person assigned to you was combing through your bank records.

That person's assignment is to research new inductees. Whoever it was may have seen a pattern in the things you've purchased on the establishments you've eaten in. From that, they begin to build your likes and dislikes."

"Wow. Amazing." I say. I'm totally amazed.

"If a researcher sees a restaurant, we will call the restaurant and have them pull the receipt to see what exactly was ordered by the person. So someone saw that you may have ordered this particular meal more than once. From there, they begin to put two and two together and formulate the things you like to eat."

"That's amazing! Why does The Agency do all this? Are these assignments that important?"

Alexander puts his fork down. He finishes chewing whatever is in his mouth and seems to ponder his answer before he says anything. "These assignments are honestly all that this life is about. They make the world go round. Whatever assignment you get will be so important it will blow your mind. You better see it that way too because if..." He takes his phone out. It's vibrating. Alexander stops speaking to read a long text message that just came into his phone.

"Um... is something wrong?" I see that Alexander's expression has changed.

"Damn!" Alexander slams his hand on the table and puts his phone down. I don't know what to say or do. I don't know if I can ask what happened or what is going on. I'm choosing to allow him to tell me instead of asking. I'm too afraid to do anything. "I'm sorry man. Just got some bad news. Remember that guy from orientation... Frank is his name."

"Oh yeah, the older guy." I say. Of course I remember Frank. Last I saw him, he left holding his chest and crying pretty badly.

"Yeah, the old guy. He's not coming back. He cracked under the pressure." Alexander says.

"Aw man! That's bad! So... he has to go back to Hell now?" I ask.

"He's already there. So is Bernard." Alexander replies.

"Who?"

"Bernard, Frank's Chief Presenter. Remember him?"

"Oh, I never heard his name. Bernard? Why is he in Hell?"

Alexander sighs before he answers. "This is how it works. If a new inductee cracks under the pressure and doesn't complete their orientation or training, then that new inductee goes back to Hell. The Chief Presenter that is assigned to that person also goes to Hell but only for a certain period of time."

"What!"

"Yes. The Chief Presenter holds the responsibility of making sure the person doesn't crack under the pressure. If the person doesn't make it, the Chief Presenter is responsible. The first time it happens, the Chief Presenter spends three days in Hell. The second time it happens, the Chief Presenter spends three weeks in Hell. The third time it happens, the Chief Presenter spends three months in Hell. If it happens a fourth time, the Chief Presenter is terminated from The Agency and goes back to Hell forever."

I'm speechless. I don't know what to say. I'm trying to think of what to ask and cannot come up with anything.

"This is how The Agency guarantees that all Chief Presenters work their assignments to the best of their ability. None of us want to spend three seconds in Hell. To consider spending three days is a horrible thought. I have to work my assignment to make sure I don't go prematurely. So, Bernard is there now."

I now remember the look on Bernard's face earlier today when Frank was seemingly having a heart attack. The pressure was too much for Frank but Bernard was more concerned than Frank was. Bernard is now in Hell suffering because Frank won't finish orientation. Wow. The checks and balance system of The Agency is incredible.

"Do you know if this is Bernard's first time with a new inductee that won't make it through the training?" I ask.

"I'm not sure. I don't know Bernard that well so I don't know. It's probably his first. I remember last year there was a Chief Presenter who had to be restrained by the very security detail that was working with him because it was his final time. His new inductee couldn't handle it and he knew that he would be in Hell forever if that person couldn't snap out of it." Alexander says.

"So you're really hoping I do well with all of this?" I ask.

"Yeah. I am. I'm gonna do my best to make sure you do. Neither of us will go before we all have to go. Hopefully, that's thousands of years from now."

Like clockwork, Josh and Kevin were waiting outside of the new condo in the SUV. They asked if I had a restful night and I actually had. I didn't dream about going to Hell. I'm not sure if they can control when the dream happens but it didn't happen last night and I'm grateful. I did cry once I got into my new bed. As comfortable and as relaxing as the bed was, the reality did kick in. The dinner was amazing, but the reality still kicked in. The conversation with Alexander until he finally left was good. He answered so many questions for me. The reality still kicked in.

I toured every inch of my home. Every room is fully furnished. The furniture is absolutely the caliber that I like. My closet is full of designer suits. The style is the same as what I used to wear. My favorite cologne, my toothpaste, every little detail was taken care of and inserted into my new place.

Once I got into bed, I began thinking of my family and friends. Alexander said they were at my old condo retrieving my things. That makes perfect sense. Although I was told they wouldn't recognize me, its probably not the best idea for me to see them either. I began to cry as I thought about that. I wondered how Julian feels knowing that he was texting me when I had the fatal car accident. I wondered how many people will attend my funeral. I thought about people crying for me. I wonder what people are going to say about me. It became overwhelming and I started to cry. I grabbed the blanket and held it against my face and I cried so hard I could hear myself.

I thought about Frank. He couldn't take the pressure but I know he regrets not completing the orientation. He's in Hell right now. In as much emotional pain that he was experiencing yesterday, he's experiencing a billion times more pain now. According to Vince, there's no coming back for him. I know he regrets not receiving an assignment and going to work.

"Glad you had a restful night. You don't want to be sleepy in class." Kevin says.

I don't know how to respond so I don't.

"I'm sure you had a lot of questions for Alexander. He's really good with answering questions. You're lucky to have him as your CP. I've done security for other Presenters who don't have the positive attitude that Alexander does. Makes the entire first few days bad for the new inductee. If you think about all you have to deal with, the least the CP can do is to keep you positive. That way, you can fulfill your assignment and be here as long as possible." Kevin is very talkative this morning. He barely said one word in the first 24 hours of me meeting him. Now he is a talking machine.

"He did. He answered a ton of my questions while we ate. Then we sat and watched a video of Bishop H.M. Clarksdale on Youtube."

"Oh yeah! Isn't that wild that he's a coworker?" Josh says as he drives. "How was the Bishop's message?"

Bishop Clarksdale has on a power blue three piece suit. When I was working for the firm in my beforelife, I remember we would grade our clients and partner meetings by men who wore power suits. He has on a colorful tie, nice shiny shoes and French cuffs on his shirt. He has a bright yellow flower on his lapel which I think is a signature accessory to his outfits. He wears a flower all the time. I always thought his stylist must be one of the highest paid people on Bishop Clarksdale's staff.

I can't say I'm a true follower of Bishop H.M. Clarksdale. I've never been to his church nor heard him speak live. I rarely went to church in general, let alone make a special trip to visit his megachurch. Yet I've heard of thousands of people who make an annual trip to his church for a special weekend event that he does. I've heard of massive crowds when he does crusades in Africa or other foreign countries. When he travels, he draws thousands of people and fills arenas. He has authored so many books, I would have to Google him to find out how many books he's done. I remember he produced a few movies with a few very popular actors and actresses. His latest venture was something to do with a satellite but I never heard too much more about that.

When he walks onto the stage, he gets a standing ovation. He quickly quiets the crowd by lifting both hands. "I thank you, each and every one of you for hearing with your ears and your heart. Whether you're hearing live in our megacenter or via television or the internet. God loves you and so do I, welcome to the Bishop Clarksdale hour." He repeats this greeting word for word with every service. His theme music kicks in. Alexander whistles the tune.

I turn to him. "I guess you're pretty familiar with his stuff huh?"

Alexander smiles. "Well he changes the theme song every television season. I didn't watch too many of his sermons last year but I've been following more this season. You gotta admit, it's catchy."

I look at Alexander like he has three heads. I don't care how many times this situation, The Agency, or whatever else is explained to me. I will still be caught off guard with everyone's cavalier attitude. I will find it strange that these people can make jokes and operate as if life is normal. No matter how you slice it, we're all going back to that place. Alexander, me, the trainers, the security, Bishop H.M. Clarksdale, all of us. If it's today, next week or in fifty years, we're still all going to end up there. That's enough to keep me in a miserable state.

"In today's message, I want to talk to you for a few moments about feelings." Bishop Clarksdale grabs my attention and I turn back to the screen. "How many of you by a show of hands feel like your life is an emotional roller coaster? One minute you're up and the next minute you're down. One day you're experiencing a mountaintop experience and the very next day, you're feeling like you're in the bottom of the valley. Am I the only one who can be honest and say he feels that way?" Thousands of people raise their hands along with Bishop Clarksdale. "The truth of the matter, my brothers and sisters is that if we're honest with ourselves, we recognize and realize that we go through stuff. It's the stuff of life that can drive you crazy! Can I get a witness?" He pauses for a response and hears many in the crowd shout "Amen!"

The camera pans the audience at just the right time to show people eagerly anticipating his next word. His audience is a mixture of all races, ages and income levels. Everyone following along and paying close attention.

"Stuff can be overwhelming. Stuff can cause you to want to lose it all. Stuff can make you make bad decisions and lose everything you've worked hard to achieve. Stuff stuff stuff!" Someone in the audience yells out the word stuff. "I see somebody is hearing me! Your stuff can get you messed up! Your stuff can get you jacked up! Your stuff can get you... how the young folks say it today... turnt up!" Everyone begins to laugh as Bishop Clarksdale laughs at his own joke.

He steps away from his podium and begins to speak in a more casual and relaxed tone. "I was hanging out with my grandchildren the other day. You know, the twins Maya and Michael. We decide to go get something to eat so we go to Olive Garden. The one right over here off the Boulevard. So we get there and we're seated. A few minutes later, a family comes in that the twins recognize. One of their classmates comes in with her parents. Once they greet each other, Maya turns to me with those big puppy dog eyes and says 'Pop Pop, can Alison and her family sit with us?' Now she know good and well I can't say no to her!" The audience erupts in laughter. "That's why Michael didn't ask because he know I would've said Hell no!" This makes the audience laugh even harder. "So I say sure, sit with us. So what started out as a day I thought I would spend talking and exchanging with my grandkids, was replaced with the grandkids talking to Alison and Alison's parents asking me spiritual advice!" The crowd is eating this up and laughing hysterically. "Somebody say amen!" The arena erupts in unison. "So we eat and have a great time of fellowship. Then the check comes and this is how I know it's a conspiracy and God is in the conspiracy business. The waiter walks right past Alison... past Maya and Michael... past Alison's parents... and right over to me! Now what made that waiter think, that I was supposed to pick up the tab for all of God's people?" Clearly Bishop Clarksdale is joking as he has a huge smile on his face. The camera has been panning through the audience and everyone is laughing along. The camera shows the team of ministers who are a part of the church. Some are laughing, some are standing. "Here's my point. I grabbed the check and looked at Maya. She gives me the puppy dog eyes so I look over at Michael instead. Now when Michael smiles at me, it's not like how Maya smiles at me. Instead of my heart turning to mush because my baby granddaughter Maya has puppy dog eyes, my soul got turnt up! Somebody say turnt up!" A roar of "Turnt up!" comes from the arena in a thunderous way.

The camera pans on Bishop Clarkdale's grandchildren, Maya and Michael who are standing next to one another. I've seen them before. They are seated on the stage next to their grandmother, First Lady Ingrid Clarksdale.

"Let me pause here and say that Mr. and Mrs. Richardson are wonderful people and I enjoyed conversing with them. I had no problem picking up the tab at Olive Garden. Some of y'all can't take a joke and will be sending me emails all week about how rude I am. So let me just put that out there!" The audience is pleased as they applaud the story.

"Stuff can have you turnt up! So how do we best handle our stuff? What's the best way to deal with the stuff you have to deal with on a daily basis? Well there's three things I want to share with you on how best to handle your stuff so your stuff doesn't handle you. That's why I want to title this message, Handling Your Stuff!" Bishop Clarksdale has made his way back to the podium right on time to go back to his notes. "The first point I want to share in the handling of your stuff is to manage your time. Somebody say manage your time!"

Everyone in the audience responds accordingly. "Manage your time!" The camera shows someone writing the words; manage your time onto a notebook.

"Yes yes manage your time. See, the main reason we have stuff in our life is because we don't manage our time well. We sleep too late and rush in the morning. We arrive late because we didn't anticipate traffic. We're sleepy after our lunch break because we didn't prepare a healthier meal. We go to bed late because we watch the game. Listen beloved, get some rest! Get some rest! Get some rest! I'm going to keep repeating that until you get it! Get some rest! Our body is a temple and it needs rest to function properly. If you rest your body and mind, you are better at making decisions. When you make your decisions with a focused mind, you're more apt to make a better decision. So manage your time and get some rest! Amen?"

As if trained to, the audience responds with a loud and thunderous amen. "Amen!

"Number two. And I already know this gonna mess most of y'all up... drink more water! Now..." He steps away from the podium again to talk in his more relaxed tone. "...I know what y'all are already thinking. I know my congregation.

The bible says that the shepherd knows his sheep very well. I know y'all gonna say 'Well Bishop I already drink a lot of water!' Stop it! Y'all countin' your Starbucks iced cinnamon almond milk macchiato... venti!" The crowd laughs, especially when he says venti. "I knew what y'all was thinking because I see how many coffees we sell in our coffee shop before service! Don't lie to the bishop!" He laughs which causes everyone to laugh with him. "Listen. The bishop loves you and to all of you in TV and internet land," he looks directly into the camera, "I love each of you too! Drink your water! It helps your body which helps your mind. If you help your mind, you can make better decisions. If you make better decisions, you can control your stuff and not allow your stuff to control you! Am I making sense to anybody in the house?"

The entire audience seems to respond with an amen. Like clockwork, the camera pans the enormous crowd that is hanging on every word.

"The third thing, and this is probably the most important... manage your emotions! You have to keep it under control. You cannot allow your emotions to get the best of you. Instead, get the best of your emotions. If you don't want your stuff to run your life, don't allow your stuff to run your life. You sometimes have to look yourself in the mirror and say self, we're better than this! We're stronger than this! We've conquered more than this! You have to pick yourself up, dust yourself off, and fight another day! Listen, God didn't make no punks! God brought you to the situation and God will bring your through the situation! Can I get an amen?"

"Amen!"

"Preach Bishop!"

"Go head!"

"Manage yourself! Talk to yourself! Control yourself! Encourage yourself! Pray for yourself! Tell yourself you can do it! Convince yourself that you're worth more than suffering! See yourself in a better situation! Love yourself! Manage yourself! Don't let your stuff manage you!"

He raises his hands. Most of the crowd is now on their feet. Some are clapping. Some are screaming. Some are jumping up and down. All are in favor of everything he is saying. Bishop Clarksdale closes his eyes and raises his head. He's mouthing words that I can't make out. It seems as if he's praying. The video fades and ends.

"I think I may have watched that one before. That was good." Josh says. Apparently, he is a fan of Bishop. Kevin not as much as now he is quiet and Josh is doing the talking.

"Alexander broke down for me that a lot of his sermons have to do with positive thinking and basically being a good person but not with any connection with God."

"Yeah. It's a lot more than that though. The thing is, with Bishop Clarksdale, the key is for him to keep people off of their God given purpose. That's his assignment. If a person's purpose is to become a painter, and they follow Bishop Clarksdale, he will have them being a plumber. They may be happy as a plumber but they will never fulfill their purpose. That's the point. Whatever it is you were here for in your beforelife, he tries to keep you out of it. The whole ministry is very strategic."

"Alexander told me that. He told me that First Lady Clarksdale doesn't even know! I was shocked when he told me that. His own wife doesn't even know!" I say as we are driving the now familiar route to the training facility downtown.

"Yeah. She's still in her beforelife. So in her mind, she is married to this incredible preacher. This great man of God. In actuality, she is married to a man who has already died, came back to work for The Agency, built a ministry and married her. She's living an incredible lifestyle but has no idea that she is totally out of her purpose just by being connected to him." Josh seems to be a bigger fan of Bishop Clarksdale than I thought. As surprised as I was to learn of his involvement with The Agency, this information seems to be more intriguing and troubling. Why would it be so important to keep someone away from their purpose? Why is so much effort put into a person that is deceiving so many? There were thousands of people attending the Bishop's service. Alexander told me that out of all of the people who attend, less than one hundred work for The Agency. That means that thousands are still in their beforelife. They adore him and have no idea.

"Do we go into the same front door as yesterday or was that an orientation door or something?" I ask as we arrive in the parking lot.

"Same door. We just go straight to the elevators and go up to your classroom. There's a bunch of new inductees coming in today just like you did yesterday. They will be led to registration like you were. You can grab a muffin or coffee or something on the way up if you want."

As we go into the front door, there seems to be about the same number of people here as yesterday. I scan the crowd and see no one I recognize. I don't know why I thought I would recognize anyone, I only really met the people in my class.

"I think I'm gonna grab a doughnut or something. I'm learning the value of all of this good food." I tell Kevin and Josh.

"Yeah, we got a few minutes. You got time." Kevin says. "Josh you want something?"

"Yeah, I might as well go get something too."

The three of us make our way to the continental buffet.

As I get close to the table, I recognize Suzanne and her Chief Presenter. I never learned her Chief Presenter's name. I tap Suzanne on the shoulder. "Hey. Good morning."

Suzanne turns around. "Oh... um, Brian right?" she asks.

"I guess." I say.

For the first time, I see Suzanne smile. "I know. Getting used to this name. Suzanne it is."

I grab a powdered doughnut and a cup of coffee. As we make our way to the elevator, I see Alexander waiting for us.

"Ready for your first class?" Alexander asks as he pats me on the arm.

"I don't have much choice." I say.

"No you don't. Clear your mind of all preconceived notions of what you thought about humanity. You're about to learn a whole different way to see things." He says as we step onto the elevator.

"I am?"

Suzanne and I enter a classroom on the second floor after reporting in with Vince upstairs. I feel like I'm in college again. I quickly deduce that the people who were also new inductees yesterday are all placed in the same class with me now. I recognize a few of the faces that I happened to see when we were on the tour yesterday. Sheldon is here with his Chief Presenter as well. Other than Suzanne and Sheldon, I don't know which of the others in the room are new inductees or Chief Presenters. I take my seat next to Alexander, right behind Suzanne and her Chief Presenter. There is a man at the front of the classroom who shook hands with Alexander when we first entered the room.

"My name is Terry and I'm the instructor of Human Emotion and Reason. This is a four week course in which you will learn elements of the human mind that will assist you in whatever your assignment is. As you were taught yesterday, The Agency employs two types of workers. Support staff and interactive staff. In either case, a thorough understanding of the human thought process will cause you to do your job more efficiently. Through this course, you'll learn how to think differently."

Terry looks to be in his fifties. He actually looks like a professor. He has thin rimmed glasses that keep sliding down his nose. He has pushed them up at least seven times already. His appearance is sloppy as if he woke up late, didn't have a chance to iron his shirt nor tuck it in. He's wearing a black tie that is crooked and loosely around his neck. His hair doesn't seem managed. "A little background on me as your instructor, this is my thirty ninth time teaching this course. For those non mathematicians, that's a little over three years. I teach a new set of inductees every month. The only time that was disrupted was a year and a half ago when every new inductee in the class lost control and was terminated by The Agency. In the span of four weeks, we lost every single one of them back to their doom. Other than that one occurrence, things have run pretty smoothly. I have been with The Agency for four years."

Wow, an entire class of new inductees went back to Hell? Why?

"So let's get started. Human Emotion and Reason. There is a definite and strategic reason why this is the first course you take. Your role in The Agency is solely dependent upon you learning the human psyche. What you thought you knew about people is probably all wrong. We are here to reprogram your process of thought so you can better understand. By doing that, you can make calculated decisions as opposed to emotional decisions." Terry pauses and scans the room with his eyes. He pushes his glasses back up his nose and continues. "Every decision you have made in your beforelife was either based on an emotional stimulus or a time continuum. Take a moment to think about that. Everything you ever did was based on an emotion. That's incredible when you take a moment and allow that to sink in. Everything."

Terry pauses before he continues. He looks through the class of new inductees and smiles. He continues. "You know, before I get into the lesson, let me say something. In this course, I'm going to introduce you to a variety of terms and explanations. I want to start with this one. What each of you is experiencing right now is a term we call Kakoneirophobia Informa. Kakoneirophobia is the fear of nightmares or evil dreams. Everyone in this classroom has experienced the worst dream they've ever had in their beforelife. Based on that horrific nightmare, you next had to make the most difficult decision you've ever made. Informa. Technically it was a no brainer but you wish you hadn't had to make that choice. We all share in this incredible afterlife phenomenon unfortunately. Kakoneirophobia Informa is what you will wrestle with for as long as you're with The Agency. I wrestle with it and I'm the instructor. It's adjusting to what you're now dealing with. Understanding what you're dealing with however is how you will make it through in completing your assignment. It doesn't matter if your assignment is support or interactive, you will have bad days and low times as you perform your duties. Take the time to tap into your emotions so you know that you're guaranteeing yourself the longest stay possible."

"Human emotion is the basis of all of our existence. It is what kept you going in your beforelife and will sustain you until the end in your afterlife. The manner in which you deal with disappointment or success will greatly impact how you develop and become an effective Agency member. The thing we've learned about ourselves, about humans, is that our minds revolve around maximum and minimal addictions. Everyone pay attention because some of you will receive an interactive assignment and this information will be critical to your success."

I have no idea what my assignment is going to be but like everyone else, I begin to take notes.

"Humans", Terry continues, "go through a vast continuum of addictive emotions. Some are psychological, some spiritual. There are some that are financially based and some strictly emotional. Our research has shown the vast majority of the addictive behaviors are in the basic human needs. The basic human physical needs are oxygen and water. What the human heart, soul and mind need however are affection, love, encouragement, discipline, education and structure. Without each of these key elements in some degree, a person can literally lose their mind."

"In general, people live their lives in addictive mundane patterns in order to fulfill the needs that satisfy the heart, soul and mind. We at The Agency have found complete ways to manipulate the desire that we intrinsically have in order to serve our purposes. This is how we have lasted as long as we have as an organization and as individuals. With that being the backdrop, let's start with the basics."

"An emotion is a feeling or intensified mental state that arises without conscious effort. That feeling can be love, hate, joy, sorrow, courage, fear and millions of others. For every emotion, there is a counter emotion just as intense. These feelings are a result of stimulus coming into contact with one or more of the five human senses. The senses, as you probably remember, are sight, sound, taste, touch and smell. Once a stimulus comes into contact with a human through the senses, the human makes a decision. This decision is the key element of life on Earth for mankind. The first time you came into contact with a hamburger, it was introduced to your five senses. You looked at it and it may have looked delicious. You smelled it cooking and your body began to desire it. You touched it by picking it up. You tasted it and made a decision. Now, if your decision at that moment was that you hated hamburgers, that would steer your life down a particular path. You may never step foot in a fast food burger joint again. Imagine never going to McDonald's. Sounds simple but this basic example has shaped you before you even knew who you were. Everything you like or dislike is based on this simple equation of sense contact, decision and emotion. So what is the point? What is the point of this class? What is the point of you... each of you... learning this? What is the point of perfecting this? Why do you need to become a master at this?"

I know that Terry doesn't expect an answer. Everyone under the sound of his voice is too petrified to attempt to answer. He continues as he knows that no one will say anything. I certainly won't.

"The point of you mastering emotions is twofold. First, and this is very important. Write this down. You have to be in control of your emotions at all times." He pauses so everyone has enough time to write it. He then repeats it. "You have to be in control of your emotions at all times. You cannot have a breakdown as you're working your assignment. If you do, that may cause you to terminate your membership with The Agency. Focus on your assignment. Get it done. Second, especially for you with interactive assignments, you have to learn how to control the emotions of others. Manipulation may be a key element of your assignment. Without the art of controlling another person's emotional state, you may be of no use to The Agency."

His last sentence made my heart skip a beat. I feel like I can't breathe but I don't dare move. I just won't breathe. Taking in what he just said... to be of no use to The Agency means you go to Hell. No. No! I will be of great use to The Agency. I will do everything that I can to be a great asset no matter what. I don't ever want to go back.

"So how do you learn and control someone else's

emotions? I created a phrase that I want you all to write down. I coined it the Push and Pull Method. You'll learn that Agency members are open to ideas so if you have a creative idea, share it. It may become a part of the curriculum taught in one of the training classes. Due to some of my beforelife experiences, I am well versed in the areas of behavioral therapy. This led me to my assignment of teaching this course and helping others understand the way emotions work. Learning this ensures everyone's long survival with The Agency. But back to my Push and Pull Method. This is how it works. If you and I are in a relationship of any sort, a marriage, a coworker, a brother or sister, a next-door neighbor, I can manipulate you by pushing when you pull or pulling when you push. When a person displays an emotion, you counter with the opposite emotion. A person that is angry will respond better when they are met with an emotional response of comfort. So they put out anger, I put out comfort. Since these emotions are somewhat opposite of one another, its like pushing and pulling. Pushing and pulling are opposite forces in physics. However, if we push and pull at the same time, we can create seamless movement and energy. If we are sawing a huge log with a two person saw, pushing and pulling together become essential. Therefore, you have to learn the emotions and what the counterparts are."

Terry opens a small black book. He turns to a page and begins to read. "For I have not given you a spirit of fear, but of power and of love and of a sound mind." He closes the book. "Some of you may have heard that expression before. Let's break down that sentence. Fear. Power. Love. Sound mind. One emotion is on one side of the spectrum. Three emotions are on the other side. Push and Pull Method. When a person exhibits fear, and you don't want them to go in that direction, you exhibit a sound mind. When a person exhibits fear and it leads them in the direction that you want them to go, then you continue with a co-emotion like anxiety. It all depends on where you want to take the relationship in that moment."

Terry picks up another book and holds it up. "Each of you will receive a copy of this book. It is your new bible. It is a list of every emotion and the definition of it. That is the first half of the book. The second half of the book is the counter emotions list. You have to learn this book. Over the next four weeks, we will be reading from this book and committing these to memory." In the next moment, I see two men and two women carrying stacks of the little emotion books. They begin passing out books at the end of each row in order for us to pass down until everyone has one. When I get mine, I open it and page through it quickly. It's set up like a dictionary. I put it down as Terry continues with the class.

"You will be required to learn the emotional terms listed on my class website. The link is provided on page seven of the book you just received. Over the next few weeks, we will break all of these down so you will have a thorough understanding of each of the emotions you will see while working your assignment."

He pauses. When the new inductees realize that Terry has stopped talking, they all look up from their emotion handbook. Everyone was paging through it like I was. We see Terry standing in front... no words... no movements. "Now that I have your attention again, are there any questions?" No one says one word. "Of course not. Let me tell you why none of you will ask a question. Each of you can think of one thousand questions to ask right now yet no one will say anything. Open your handbook and turn to page three." He waits for each person to do it. "The emotions in the book are not listed in alphabetical order. They are listed instead by level of importance. The reason none of you asked a question when given the opportunity a few seconds ago is listed on page three. It is an intense emotion called terror. Terror causes reactions in your body that can paralyze you in an instant. It is a different level of fear. Terror is a more intense level of fear. Look at what it says in your book. Terror is a state of intense fear. The emotional state of terror evokes an aspect of fright and anxiety. The result of terror can be devastatingly lasting." Everyone looks up from page three as Terry speaks freely. "Do you realize an act of terror on a community will change the history of that community forever? That community can be a local school, a district, a state or even a country. The aftermath of an act of terror has lingering affects that can last one hundred years. Think about how nine eleven affected the United States. That was an act of terror. Think of Pearl Harbor. Think of Hiroshima and Nagasaki. I can list acts of terror for the next hour and the exact emotion displayed that day is what you're feeling right now. That's why no one volunteers to ask a question. You're petrified by terror."

"Now turn to page three seventy four." Terry waits for everyone to turn to that page. "Now let's look at the counter to terror. There's only one emotion that can counter an emotion as intense as terror. Look at the first emotion in the counter emotion section. It's love. Love is a combination of many emotional feelings that can be as simple as pleasure and as complex as deep affection. Love is the emotion responsible for the continuation of the human race. It is the absolute strongest of all emotions. Love encompasses a variety of other emotions at times and can overshadow any other emotion. Love is the only spirit emotion strong enough to overshadow the spirit of terror."

"Ladies and gentlemen, over the next four weeks, we're going to learn every emotion known to mankind. We're going to study them and restudy them. We're going to remember them, forget them, then remember them again. The one thing I can guarantee each of you is this... by the end of this four week session, you will remember every single emotion in this book like the back of your hand. How can I say that so confidently? I can say that with confidence because terror awaits anyone who doesn't accomplish that task. It is my assignment to guarantee each of you pass this course. I will accomplish my assignment with flying colors."

Terry takes his glasses off as he puts his book down. "Remember when this class began, I mentioned that an entire class failed and was sent to their doom? As a part of my assignment, I went with then. I spent ninety days in Hell as a consequence of my training being a failure. From the moment I rejoined The Agency after that ninety day punishment, I took my assignment a lot more serious. It was then that I wrote this handbook. I came up with the Push and Pull Method. I wrote the curriculum for this course. I did the research by staying up night and day. My goal was to never go back to that place until that time that I have no choice. As long as I have a choice, I will work my assignment. What is motivating me to work so hard you ask? I'll tell you. Terror. The spirit of terror is what is motivating me. What I went through for ninety days was nothing short of the worst terror humanly imaginable. I remember every second of that ninety day nightmare... I guarantee, it won't happen again. With that... that ends today's class. Welcome to Human Emotion and Reason."

According to my tablet, our second course starting today is in an auditorium on the third floor. After checking in with Vince upstairs, I approach the auditorium. There seems to be an unusually large crowd waiting to go inside. Maybe they're combining classes. Until now, I've never seen this many inductees in any one setting. Even lunch is very controlled as to how many people are eating lunch at the same time. This however seems to be hundreds more people. Once the doors open I walk in with everyone else. The auditorium is huge. From a quick glance, this place can seat five hundred people easily.

"Good morning. My name is Dr. Reynolds. I'm your instructor for The Fall of Life and the Fall of Man course. In The Agency, I'm one of very few Instructor Priests. There are only 1,000 IPs in the entire agency. This class is scheduled each year and takes place only twice per year in this location. That is why this class is better attended than the other class you started four weeks ago. Once we complete the course, I will be travelling to Dubai to teach it there. The IPs rotate from location to location teaching the course." Dr. Reynolds is a severely overweight Asian man. For a man his size, he seems to dress well. His suit is clearly tailor made.

I did notice that there are students in this class that I have never met before. Some I have seen in passing when we walk into the building. Most I have never seen. There seems to be a melting pot of races and genders. The class is probably split fifty percent male and fifty percent female. There are young people, old people, middle age people. Death respects no one.

"When you take the course on the various roles and

departments in The Agency, you'll hear about the IP position. I'll still explain it now since I'm probably the only one you're going to meet until you start your assignments. Most IPs in The Agency worked in some sort of leadership capacity in a religious organization in their beforelife. For me, I was an assistant pastor of a small church. The other profession that leads to an afterlife as an IP is any profession that deals with history like a history professor or an archivist."

"Historians see the world in a totally different light. Therefore, they are able to relay information differently. It's truly a gift. Most historians and religious leaders are story tellers. We have an uncanny ability to relay a message in a way that anyone at almost any age can get it and understand it. My role here as your IP for the next few weeks is vitally important to each of your individual success rates here at The Agency."

Dr. Reynolds pauses and looks around the completely filled arena. "Let me ask a question before we get started. How many people in this room want to avoid going to Hell for as long as humanly possible?" I don't know whether I should raise my hand or not but everyone shoots their hands up. One guy has both hands up. I raise my hand and realize that everyone in the room has a hand in the air. "Your success in totally understanding what I will teach you over the next four weeks will absolutely assist you in staying on Earth for a long time. A very, very long time!" One man in the audience starts to clap and others join in. Dr. Reynolds waits for the applause to die down before he continues. "Pay very close attention to the things I teach you in this course. These things will help you. The more you understand the environment you've been placed in, the better you can work your role as a member of The Agency."

As Dr. Reynolds says that, he presses a button on a remote control that I didn't notice is in his hand. The lights dim and a huge screen slowly lowers from the ceiling. As soon as it has fully lowered, he clicks a button and a slide is projected onto the screen that says The Fall of Life and The Fall of Man.

"The first part of the course is a historical look at the spirit world. You exist a lot more cognizant of spirits now that you exist in an afterlife state. Therefore, a full understanding of what surrounds you is necessary for you to work your assignment to the best of your ability. All ministering spirits were created at the same time by the same being. Although they were created at the same time..."

As Dr. Reynolds speaks, the first slide shows lights all over the screen that resemble stars in the midnight sky.

"...they were not created the same or with the same responsibility. Each spirit, or light as seen here on the screen, is designated to a particular assignment. No human can ever perform an assignment to the perfection of a spirit. In that sense, the spirits dominate the fortitude of any human being. Where human beings excel over spirits is in the area of emotions. Spirits don't have the emotional make up of any of you. Something that may make you or I cry won't move a spirit in the least bit. They are focused on their assignment and that's basically it for them."

"Assignments were given out by the one being that created all spirits. Some spirits were created to serve. Other spirits were created for work. Other spirits were created to protect."

The next slide has an outline of words: Cherubim, Seraphim, Ministering Angels, and Archangels.

Here are the major categories of spirits before the fall of man. Each group has a distinct assignment and many spirits within a particular category have assignments within their assignments. So first, the Cherubim."

"I see other people take out their personal tablets to take notes. I already had mine out. I've always been a very meticulous note taker. I know the importance of small details. I never missed a beat in the things I found myself involved with in my beforelife. I take that even with a more serious vigor now. I never saw the details of my life as a matter of life or death but now I see these things I'm learning as a differing factor between success and failure. Failure speeds up the inevitable that no one in this entire crowded arena wants to face. If Jesus waits ten million millenniums before He returns that would still be too soon.

"The Cherubim are a sect of spirit lights that were created to guard and protect. You won't encounter Cherubim but it's good to know what they are and what they are assigned to do. When one is placed on an assignment to guard something, it is almost impossible to break through them."

Dr. Reynolds pulls up a slide. The slide shows a huge creature. It looks like it's twenty feet tall. Some people in the room gasp. The creature has four wings and what looks like multiple heads. I know I see a lion head and an eagle head as two of the heads on it. It looks both disgusting and majestic. I can't stand to look at it but I can't seem to turn away.

"These are the gatekeepers. If any of you ever grew up in church or heard bible stories and remember the story of Adam and Eve, then you heard of the Cherubim. Remember in the story when Adam and Eve got in trouble with God and they were kicked out of the Garden of Eden?" He shows a slide of two people wearing leaves as clothes, the depiction we all think of when we think of Adam and Eve. "When they were kicked out of the Garden of Eden, we were told that an angel was placed at the gate so they couldn't get back in. What we weren't told in the story is what that angel looked like. Well here it is folks and trust me when I tell you, when you see this guy breathing heavy and staring at you, you don't want to confront him. If you remember the story correctly, he carried a sword of fire which he could swing in any direction. He's not one to be messed with! Now imagine Adam and Eve trying to get past this guy to get back into the Garden and back to the original tree!"

I don't know about Adam and Eve but ain't no human alive bad enough to get past that thing! I know I'm not. I wouldn't go anywhere near that.

"Now the Seraphim. This group of lights operate on a different assignment. They are specifically here to talk." Dr. Reynolds stops and looks at the totally confused audience. He then laughs. "You look confused. No, I didn't stutter. Seraphim are spirits in a class by themselves. They talk... a lot!"

He clicks his remote to show a new slide. This slide depicts what looks like a man with wings. The image on the screen is what most people would consider a typical angel.

"This is a Seraphim. As you can see, he has wings and can

fly." He changes slides. Now the same angel has another set of wings. "These spirits are unique. Not only do they have wings protruding from their back in which they use to fly but they also have a pair of wings that are used to cover their eyes..." he clicks the slide again, "and a pair to cover their feet. Six wings in all." The slide now shows the Seraphim in motion. He is hovering in the air by flapping the first set of wings that I saw. The other sets of wings he is using to cover his eyes and feet. "When I said that this angel talks a lot, all they do is fly around and say three words. All day... every day... every weekend... all night... all the time." Dr. Reynolds exaggerates his words for emphasis but no one seems amused. We're all either in shock of what we're going through or in shock of what we're being taught. "The Seraphim repeat the phrase 'He is holy!' all day. They say it to each other. That's all they say. You'll never encounter them, they never leave heaven."

"Now, for a set of angels that you actually will encounter... the Ministering Angels. This group has the task of fulfilling orders. In other words, they may receive an order to do something and they are very efficient in fulfilling their tasks. As we describe these angelic beings in our upcoming classes, you're going to probably learn the most about this particular group. Although the Archangel lesson is the most important to know, the Ministering Angels are the most important to understand. Let me show you why."

Dr. Reynolds clicks his remote and the next slide is an image of Jesse Buchanan. I remember Jesse Buchanan from when I was young and used to go to the dollar matinee at the movie theater with my friends. When Jesse became famous as a child actor, we all wanted to be him. He defined the role of Super Electro Boy which led to a tremendous franchise of merchandise, comics, spin off movies and an amusement park. Who could ever forget when he grew up and became Super Electro Man and adults and kids were sitting in the same theater watching the boy become a man in superhero form? Everyone knows Jesse Buchanan and how he tragically died in a plane crash on his 31st birthday.

"Who knows who this little boy is? If you know his name, just say it out loud." Everyone in the large auditorium says Jesse Buchanan in unison. "Right. This is child star Jesse Buchanan. He was a tremendous actor with a stellar career from his childhood. For those who weren't counting, Jesse starred in seventeen movies, mostly superhero related. Who could ever forget Super Electro Boy right?" There are many verbal responses from the new inductees seated in the audience. "We all remember the tragic death of Jesse when he and his friends died on a plane as he was flying to celebrate his birthday. Remember that?" Everyone responds as they should. His death was major television news. It was on every station for over a week. It felt like a national day of mourning when he died. I felt bad even though I had obviously never met him. I felt like I knew him because I grew up watching and idolizing him. Dr. Reynolds continues. "Folks, Jesse Buchanan was a Ministering Angel."

There are gasps all over the auditorium. I probably joined in the chorus of gasps myself as Dr. Reynolds begins to explain. "The Ministering Angels receive assignments to operate on Earth and interact with humans. They can never reveal that they are angels. They aren't allowed to use any type of supernatural power. Although they see the spirit realm like I'm going to teach you to do, they are limited in what they can or cannot do. So let's discuss Jesse Buchanan and let me make it make sense for you."

My mouth is literally wide open. This is absolutely unbelievable. I want to look around the auditorium to see if anyone else looks as stunned as I am but I can't take my eyes off Dr. Reynolds. This overweight man in the great suit has just captured the attention of hundreds of people with a single slide. Two minutes ago, we were all taking notes and learning the role of Seraphim light spirits. Now, there isn't a single note being taken nor a muscle moving. Everyone is fixated on this IP on stage and what he is teaching.

"Jesse Buchanan did not die a painful death. He had an assignment and he completed it. Would anyone like to guess what his assignment was?" No one moves. "I never get anyone to bite on that question when I ask it in these classes." Dr. Reynolds laughs at his own statement. I then see out of the corner of my eye a hand slowly raise. It's Suzanne.

Dr. Reynolds sees her hand in the crowd and smiles. "Yes ma'am. Finally, someone brave enough to attempt an answer! What do you think Jesse Buchanan's assignment was?"

Suzanne stands up. "I was Jesse Buchanan's biggest fan by far. I cried real tears when he died in that plane crash. I had posters of Jesse all over my walls growing up. I was the wife he never met." A light laugh fills the room of otherwise tense people living in an afterlife avoiding an eternal punishment. "If I had to think of an assignment for him, it must have been to bring joy to the world. He did that through his movies." Suzanne takes her seat.

"That's an interesting answer! Thank you for the courage to share it. No, that wasn't his assignment actually. What Jesse did when he wasn't acting... and if you're his biggest fan you may know this... he visited hospitals. Most people thought he was a humanitarian and liked to visit sick kids. He did do that. But that was a bi product of his actual mission. When Jesse would go into a hospital, he had a name that he was given. He would visit one hundred people in a particular hospital looking specifically for one or two names. The people that he looked for were on a list given him by his assigner. The names on the list he was given were of people who were dying. They may have had a few days or even a few hours left in their beforelife. Jesse would try his best to convert the person so they could avoid going to Hell or joining The Agency in the afterlife. Jesse Buchanan was extremely successful at his assignment and one of the greatest enemies The Agency has ever faced."

What? Jesse Buchanan was considered an enemy to The Agency? I guess it makes sense based on that explanation. He was trying to keep people from the fate that I now face! I wish I had met him before I died!

"Our sources tell us that before his assignment ended, Jesse Buchanan released 18,419 people from being cast into Hell. He is what is called a Ministering Angel. You would never had known if you had met him. He looked like a regular guy. In your beforelife, if you ever walked up and saw him, he looked like this..."

Dr. Reynolds shows a slide of Jesse in a photo with a few smiling fans.

"Now however, you are in the afterlife and you'll start

to see things differently. You will learn to see things in the spirit realm. So if you saw Jesse in this same photo through your spirit afterlife eyes, he looks like this..."

The next slide is the exact same picture except that Jesse is glowing with an orange glow. "This is how you can tell when a person isn't a person. This is the look of a Ministering Angel. You will all have to learn how to see things and operate in this realm. If not, these spirit beings will be obstacles to you if you're assigned an interactive assignment. They will do all that they can to stop you. We will teach you ways to work around them, based on what your assignment is. Once you see the orange glow, you know exactly who you're dealing with."

"Here are a few more people who you may have seen in your before life that were actually Ministering Angels." Dr. Reynolds starts to click the remote control. One after the other there are people that each person in this room recognizes. There are athletes, politicians, musicians and more actors. Males and females are represented. All races are represented. With each passing slide, there are more gasps from the audience. Each one is a surprise. Each surprise is more surprising than the last surprise. "Ministering Angels are everywhere. You will see them as you begin to use your spiritual senses."

He clicks to the next slide. "Let me tell you what their limitations are." The slide lists the limitations. Each person quickly grabs their tablet and starts to type the list of things. I instead take the tablet and take a picture of the huge screen. I can study the picture that I just took later today. "Ministering Angels are never allowed to attack afterlife individuals. So you will never have to face fear of physical attack. They aren't allowed. Number two, Ministering Angels are not allowed to tell a beforelife individual that they are a Ministering Angel. Now this is the most important limitation and what we use to our favor. The only reason this limitation isn't listed first is because we want all new inductees to know that you don't have to fear an angel. They won't hurt you in that sense. What they will do is attempt to hinder your assignment." I think I need to ask Alexander about these Ministering Angels and what his thoughts are on what they do. Dr. Reynolds continues. "The fact that a Ministering Angel can never reveal to a beforelife human that he or she is an angel is a great asset to our mission. Just imagine if you had a coworker in your beforelife that came to you one day and said 'Hey so and so, don't walk through that door! I'm an angel and I know what's on the other side through the spirit of prophecy!' Everyone laughs at the exaggerated tone that Dr. Reynolds uses in his description. You would either think your coworker was joking, crazy or you would call Human Resources on them." Everyone laughs but what he just said is very true. "Which of those three options you would actually do depends on the nature of the relationship that you have with that coworker. Nevertheless, there's one thing you wouldn't do. You wouldn't believe them. That is the point! Through this course, I'm going to teach you how to use that to your advantage. Humans make many decisions based on what they choose to believe or not believe. We have to learn to use that to help us fulfill our assignments and stay on Earth longer."

"Now let me explain what Ministering Angels can do. Ministering Angels are thrown into action by one of two things. Either they receive a direct assignment which comes from God or they are activated by the vocal cords of humans."

What?

Dr. Reynolds changes from his slide presentation to a video. "I need to explain how the human vocal cord can manipulate a spiritual being to work. To do that, I have to put it in context. Pay close attention to this video and when it's done, I will continue. It's only two minutes so don't fall asleep." He smiles but no one is sleeping through this. This is fascinating and terrifying. The video begins in what looks like an open grass field. The scene shows a beautiful landscape of grass, hills and trees in the distance. With light music playing in the background, the camera slowly approaches the trees. Once close enough, each tree shows hanging fruit. What catches my attention however is the type of fruit on these trees. The apples on the apple tree are the reddest apples I've ever seen. The same goes for the other trees. The largest bananas, the ripest looking oranges, multiple colored grapes on several vines. Once the camera passes all of the gorgeous fruit trees, we see a waterfall that pours into a calm lake. The camera spins upward quickly which almost makes me dizzy. The adjustment is so fast that I hear a few people jump back in their seat. When the camera comes back down, there are animals in the same area where the camera just showed plush grass. Now, within a matter of seconds, there seems to be thousands of animals. I see every animal imaginable from lions to elephants to dogs to giraffes. Every creeping crawling thing is shown in this video. Every bird from eagles to pigeons. Animals are all over the place. I see that no animal is fighting or eating any other animal. They are laying around. Some are laying on top of others. I notice an antelope playfully nudging a cheetah. Normally a cheetah would chase an antelope and devour it. In this scene, they seem to be playing. All at once, each animal rises from its lying position. At the same time, every bird that's flying comes out of the sky and lands on the ground. At the same time, every single animal bows its face down like they are bowing before a king. Then the image of a man walks toward them as if he was behind the camera the entire time. All of the animals are bowed down before this man. The video fades to black and Dr. Reynolds walks to the front of the stage.

"Ladies and gentleman that is the environment that the world was created in. That man at the very end of the video is Adam. That place is Eden. When Eden was created, it was created by the vocal cords of God. When God spoke the creation, it became. God is a speaking spirit. The only thing that God made that was not spoken was Adam. Instead of speaking Adam, God put his hands into the dirt and formed Adam. Everything else was spoken. The entire universe was spoken. God then gave Adam an incredible amount of authority. The first assignment given to a human was nomenclature. Adam was instructed to name the animals. Whatever name Adam came up with became the name of that animal. This is because God made Adam in his own image and since God is a speaking spirit, Adam is a speaking spirit. The voice of God and the voice of the humans were created to be equal for the purpose of authority. Each voice has control over both the physical world and the spirit world. When a spirit hears the vibration of the voice of God, the spirit has to submit and obey to what God says. The same was said of Adam in the beginning. The original design of man was to express vocally the assignments of God and have the spirits and creation submit and obey. What happened next is the basis of this class. The fall of man."

At that moment, the lights in the auditorium come up

and the screen begins to rise back into the ceiling. "That concludes day one of my course. We pick up tomorrow with the fall of man and what that has to do with each of you on assignment. Thank you and I will see you tomorrow."

"I have a question. This glow that Dr. Reynolds spoke about with Jesse Buchanan. Can you guys see people with a glow?" Alexander, Kevin and Josh are in the SUV with me driving back to my new home. I've been pondering this among a lot of other things since the class today. I usually ask Alexander questions over dinner at my place but this time I wanted to get Josh and Kevin's opinion as well.

Alexander responds. "It takes some training. You'll get that. Once you do, you'll be able to see them everywhere."

There is a moment of silence as I look out of the car window. I break the silence with my next question. "Can you look outside and see if you see anybody now?" I ask.

"Um, let me see." Alexander says. He and Josh look out of their windows. Kevin is driving. "OK look. Right there. See that lady right there?" Alexander is pointing at a woman at the bus stop. African American woman who looks to be in her fifties. To me, she looks like a normal person.

"The lady in the blue dress?" I ask.

"Yeah. She's a Ministering Angel."

"Yup." Josh adds.

"Wow. She looks normal. Unbelievable!" I say.

"I can show you where a lot of them are if you want to see them. We got time?" Kevin speaks for the first time.

"Yeah, go ahead." Alexander gives him permission.

Kevin takes a left turn at the light which takes us off

the course to my place. As he drives toward the other side of town I stare out the window. I see places I've seen millions of times yet now look a lot different. I'm staring at every person I see whether they are walking, standing, or driving. I'm trying to see this mysterious spiritual glow and I see nothing but people. Kevin drives into a particular neighborhood that I rarely visit. This part of town called Duncan Square is the bad part of town. Lower income residents which lends to subpar schools and inferior living conditions. Someone of my status would never spend significant time here. Although I wasn't born into money, I had made a success of my beforelife. For the most part, I lived a good life. I had plenty of money. I lived in a beautiful part of town in an expensive duplex condo. I ate well. I dressed well. I travelled well. I was a single guy living a great life. The entire time, I never knew my soul was headed to Hell and I would be conflicted as I take an assignment for The Agency in order to prolong it.

"You ever been over this way before?" Kevin asks.

"Yeah but not really. I don't frequently come to this part of town." I respond.

"You ever heard of New Hope?" he asks.

"The homeless shelter?"

"Yeah."

"Yeah, my firm hooked up with them each year to bring Thanksgiving dinners to the residents. That's probably the most amount of time I would spend out here. I came to the event three years in a row." I say. The New Hope Homeless Facility is in the heart of Duncan Square. It's a small brick building which is open to anyone who finds themselves on the streets. People who stay there get a cot, a blanket and a pillow. It's always overcrowded and the place smells bad.

Kevin turns onto 7th Street and pulls over. The New Hope Homeless Facility is across the street toward the middle of the block. There are approximately fifteen or twenty people outside the facility. Most are just sitting on the steps talking. Some are standing closer to the curb. A few men are playing a card game. Kevin turns the SUV engine off.

"OK look. How many people do you see right there?" Kevin asks.

"Looks like about fifteen or twenty I guess." I say.

"Right. Out of all those people, only two are human in the beforelife." He says.

"What?" I say as I look closely again.

"The rest are angels. They're probably waiting on particular people to come back to the shelter so they can do whatever they're supposed to do with them." Alexander says.

"Wow! I'm amazed. I don't see one glowing person!" I say.

"Right and I see several." Josh mentions. "The entire front of the building is lit up. Looks like Christmas lights to me."

I'm amazed at this spiritual phenomenon that I can't even see. Embracing the afterlife on Earth can be viewed in a myriad of ways. The obvious would be to avoid the consequence for as long as possible. Along with that come curiosity, intrigue and questions. I'm fascinated by what I'm learning even though I'm heartbroken that I have to learn it. If I had a choice to have learned of an alternative to this particular afterlife and not have to be privy to any of this, I would choose it wholeheartedly.

"Why are they gathered here? How did you know so many would be here?" I ask Kevin.

"They do a lot of work with the homeless." Kevin says.

Alexander continues Kevin's statement. "Homeless people tend to lose hope and let go of any dreams or visions they had. If they don't take their own lives, they just exist without completing any real purpose. Everyone that is born is created with a purpose. Every person's job is to find out what that purpose is and fulfill it. If a group of people aren't coming into their purpose because of a circumstance, then that would be a problem. So if homelessness is one of the causes that keeps people from their purpose, then I can see a lot of work being done to change that."

"How does that work with people like us though?" I ask.

"Oh, you can believe that members of The Agency are assigned to this issue. I'm sure there are agency members in the facility posing as someone homeless. Listen, for every measure, there is a countermeasure. If a Ministering Angel goes right, we go left. We find ways to fight the enemies of The Agency." Alexander says.

Alexander's words shock me into silence. Kevin starts the truck and drives past the homeless shelter. As we pass the facility, I take one final glance to see if I see anyone glowing. I don't.

Dr. Reynolds jumps right into today's class as if he's excited to teach it. "Archangels. Three of them. Very important to know who they are. You'll never meet them... which is good for you. Each archangel has a specific responsibility. Each is the best at his craft. No one does what they do better than an archangel. No one!" Dr. Reynolds almost screams this point into the microphone. If nothing else, he has everyone's full attention as he begins today's presentation.

"Archangel Michael." Dr. Reynolds' first slide is a massively muscular man. He is holding a huge sword in one hand and a spear in the other. He looks to have two swords on his back. He has a breastplate that looks like iron on his chest. He has more muscles in his arm than I have in my entire body. "Michael is the angel of war. When warfare breaks out in the spirit world, Michael is behind the force. Think of him as a General over millions of troops. This image isn't actually Michael. None of us have ever seen him. This is a visual description that one of our artists rendered based on information we have obtained about him. Stories have been told of Michael in war. Michael can handle slaying an army by himself."

He changes the slide. "Archangel Gabriel." This slide shows a man in a pair of jeans and a hoodie. "Believe it or not, this is our best depiction of Gabriel the mighty archangel. Gabriel is responsible to deliver messages. He talks to humans on a regular basis. The reason we depicted him in this attire is because he adjusts to whatever environment he is placed in. If he is assigned to deliver a message to someone in India, he will wear clothes appropriate for that destination. If he is to deliver a message to someone in New York City and the year is 1906, he will wear clothes that were appropriate for that time and place. He is fluent in every language. He has communicated some of the greatest messages known to mankind."

"The archangel Lucifer." This slide shows a man wearing a blue robe. On the robe are white stars and musical notes. "Lucifer was the chief musician. He was made of melodies. He was constructed as harmony. He has perfect pitch. Every time he moved, music was heard. Lucifer has occupied every sound you have ever heard. Every musical note was crafted especially for him. Every cymbal and brass instrument along with every string, every percussive, you name it or think of it, it was created for him. Just think of him as music. Imagine hearing someone speak and you fall in love with the sound of their voice. That was Lucifer. Legend has it, he was beautiful to look at and listen to. He was the most beautiful of the angels. He was also the best sounding." Dr. Reynolds changes his tone as he continues. He has calmed down from his introduction to today's class. "It is because of the brilliance of Lucifer that we have The Agency today. His genius allows us all the opportunity to stay on Earth as long as possible. He is the architect of this massive organization. He is the executive who puts all of this together. Without him, we would be in a much worst situation right now."

"As mentioned, you will never meet the archangels. You wouldn't want to be in a fight with Michael so that is to your benefit. Gabriel only speaks to people in the beforelife so you'll never meet him either. Lucifer... you'll never meet him. Trust me, you wouldn't want to."

"It's extremely important to understand them and remember their roles as it pertains to your assignment.

Not so much Lucifer but definitely the other two. Why? Beforelife humans get help from Ministering Angels and other angels as well. If a human needs warfare on their behalf, who do you think will come to their aid? It very well may be a Ministering Angel but that Ministering Angel may be in Michael's army. You need special training to know how to deal with that and many of you may be taking additional training courses on this once you receive your assignment. Gabriel delivers messages all the time. You may have an assignment and a message may be delivered to that person from Gabriel himself or an angel on his team. You would need specific instructions on how to handle that as well."

The screen fades to black. "Dealing with spirits on this side of life is a unique and special gift. It can be difficult at first but the more you interact with humans, the more you will be able to depict and understand spirits. Humans and spirits don't think the same way. Soon you will be able to pick out a spirit just by what that spirit may say or do. At least with the Ministering Angels, the glow gives them away. You'll learn how to see the glow too. It just takes focus and attention to your spiritual nature."

"For some of you, your assignment will be behind a computer screen. If that is your assignment, then none of this will really matter. Many of you will become Chief Presenters. If that is you, you will need to learn this in order to guide your new inductee through some of the things they may see. For some of you, you will absolutely need this. If your assignment causes you to interact directly with a beforelife human, then take good notes!"

"The fall of man." Dr. Reynolds says.

Dr. Reynolds is dressed in another great suit. Today he stands at a podium as he addresses the standing room only crowd. Over the past two nights, I considered every word he said over the past two days. The thing about the different classes of angels is quite interesting. The Ministering Angels that I cannot see kept me up most of the night. I still find it hard to believe that a kid actor who was adored by millions of people wasn't even human. The New Hope homeless shelter and the number of angels there. This is all incredible. I wonder how many people in my beforelife that I've interacted with are angels. I wonder if any of my former coworkers are angels. I wonder if any of my friends or fraternity brothers are. Well, maybe not my frat brothers but maybe someone in my own family.

"I hope that I've peaked your interest enough that you will be ready to receive all that I have to share with you today about the fall of man." Dr. Reynolds begins. "Let's get right into it. As we stated yesterday, Adam was given the task of naming the animals and all living beings. He was presented the creature, the creature bowed down, Adam named it. Whatever Adam said became the name. This is because Adam had authority over every living thing. His vocal chords had such power that whatever he said... happened. This was a great level of authority that Adam had that I doubt he understood. Looking back in hindsight, we can study the power in the authority that he had. We can research and dissect what it meant to have such power in a simple spoken word. Placing ourselves in his position at that time however, it's difficult to assume he realized such power. Had he realized the power that he had, the sequence of events that followed may not have happened the way that they did."

Dr. Reynolds steps away from the podium and walks to the front of the stage. He folds his arms in front of his chest and continues. "So let me ask a question and see if anyone was really paying attention yesterday." He looks around the room with a slight grin as if he is looking for a candidate to answer his question. "Can a ministering angel or a Seraphim or even a Cherubim command animals or activate the spirit world now?" There is a silence in the room. "Let me rephrase. If a ministering angel was in this room right now... and trust me, there aren't... could he or she say something using the power in their vocal chords to command another spirit to do something?" After a brief silence, a White man in the front of the room raises his hand. Dr. Reynolds points to him. "Yes sir!"

"No."

Dr. Reynolds laughs. "Of course you're gonna say that. Can you explain why not?" The man doesn't answer.

"At least you were brave enough to try to answer." Dr. Reynolds walks back behind the podium. "The gentleman who answered the question answered correctly. The answer is no. No spirit has the power or authority in their voice to activate the spirit realm. The reason they do not is because that power was first given to Adam for use by humans only. That power was then taken from Adam by the Chief Archangel whose name was Lucifer. Once Lucifer abducted the power that was given to Adam, he quickly shared it with other spirits. He designated authority the way he saw fit and this became the genesis of The Agency."

"I know each of you heard a little about the history of The Agency in your orientation session. What I'm sharing with you now is a little more detailed. The Agency began and continues as a countermeasure in the spirit realm. Whatever one side does, the other side does as a countermeasure. This has been done since the beginning and will continue to be done until the end. We in the afterlife who have chosen to work with The Agency have come to embrace the turmoil that this is."

Choosing to embrace this turmoil is an interesting spin on the existence we now are apart of. Whatever makes it more comfortable I guess. Ultimately, we're all on borrowed time.

Dr. Reynolds continues. "The Agency literally begins with the power stolen from mankind. Man no longer had the ability to speak to a spirit and cause it to submit. Man no longer had the ability to show authority over wildlife. Man no longer had the ability to speak life or death over plant life and vegetation. The spirits however did and they exercised this power often. The power was finally taken away from the spirit realm at the event known as the resurrection. When Jesus transferred from beforelife to afterlife and back to beforelife, he did so in order to reclaim the power that had been lost by humans. Never again was that power given to the spirits. So to explain the answer to my question, a ministering angel does not have the power or authority to speak things into existence because of what I just explained."

Dr. Reynolds picks up his remote control and turns to face his screen. He shows an image of a baby.

"Let me show you who now has the ability, authority and power to command spirits. These babies. These babies do." His next images are young children playing. "These children. These children do. Teenagers. Young adults." With each category he mentions, an accompanying image is displayed. "Humans in the beforelife have the ability. It was given to them in the beginning and it was given back to them. The problem with humans in the beforelife, including all of us at one time... none of us knew we had access to that kind of authority. If we did, we wouldn't be seated in this room."

Dr. Reynolds' words sting like an army of killer bees just attacked me. Words like this absolutely remind us of where we are. I don't know how anyone can be jovial with this looming over their heads. Members of The Agency however, seem to come to work as if none of this is happening. I see them laughing in the hallways or enjoying lunch. Alexander continues to tell me to make the most of my days and to not let the thoughts of what is to come consume me. He makes comments like it is imperative to shift your focus. Otherwise, you will be sent to Hell too early. I remember when he asked me how I would feel if I couldn't handle the pressure of my assignment and was sent to Hell tomorrow, then find out that Jesus doesn't return for eight million more years. Promising and terrifying at the same time.

"The interesting thing however," Dr. Reynolds continues, "is knowing this information now can assist you in your afterlife assignment. Remember this, write this down, put in on your fridge, and commit this to memory. You no longer have the ability to cause a spirit to submit with your voice but you do have the ability to influence a beforelife human that does have the ability. Let me give you an example." He stares into the crowd and points to a woman seated in the second row. "You. Please stand up and tell me your name."

The woman hesitates and doesn't move.

"It's okay. I just want to ask you a general question to prove a point. Don't be afraid. It's okay."

With these words, she slowly stands. "My name is... well my new name is Johniece."

"Thank you for our courage Johniece. Now let me ask you a very general question. Did sickness run in your family?"

"Yes." she timidly says.

"Okay. So let's say," he looks up to address the entire audience, "that this woman and I were having a conversation. She is in the beforelife and I am in the afterlife working for The Agency. Remember, I don't have the ability in my vocal chords to influence the spirit realm like she does. Once I am in the afterlife, I lose that ability. She still has it but probably doesn't realize it. So if I say out of my mouth that sickness runs in my family, it means nothing. If she however says sickness runs in her family, it becomes a declaration."

He turns back to the woman who is still standing. "So let's act as if you and I are seated in a Starbucks and are just conversing over coffee okay?"

"Okay." she replies.

"So... does sickness run in your family?"

"Yes."

"What kind of sickness specifically. Like did your

grandparents have something that passed down to your parents?"

"Well my grandmother had breast cancer. My mother did too."

"Oh wow. Same with me. High blood pressure runs in my family. I wonder why that happens like that. Did your grandmother smoke?"

"No, she wasn't a smoker. It's just something with our family I guess. I don't know. Just something about our family that it just happens."

"Okay pause!" Dr. Reynolds abruptly stops the role play. "If you're following closely to our conversation, I'm leading her to state that sickness runs in her family. If she actually admits that, although casually, I've won. My goal is to make her declare it in her own voice. Once she does, the spirit world can be activated. There is a spirit that beforelife humans call Infirmity. This spirit is activated if a beforelife human gives him authority with their voice. If my goal as a member of The Agency is to make a person sick or depressed, all I have to do is influence them to say certain things. I hope you're all paying close attention to this. This is one of the major tactics that you're going to have to perfect if you expect to perform your assignment with no glitches. Your Chief Presenter will be going over exercises with you in this area until you are comfortable talking out with someone in the beforelife."

Dinner tonight is cheese stuffed chicken breast, vegetables and rice. Afterlife culinary is outstanding. The cuisine always takes my mind off of the predicament... temporarily at least. This is the time that I get to ask Alexander whatever I want. Every night I ask him questions based on the things I learned that day. He never grows old of me inquiring about this new life we are forced to submit to. I don't know if that is his job as a Chief Presenter or him simply being accommodating but I'm glad he is so open to answer.

"I got a different kind of question for you tonight." I say in between bites.

"Oh yeah? Shoot."

"This one isn't about Dr. Reynold's class or anything like that."

"Okay. That's cool. You can ask me whatever." He replies.

"How did you die?"

Alexander pauses before he answers. He is in the middle of chewing and that may have something to do with the pause. He takes his time in chewing though so I believe he wants to get his thoughts together or would rather not answer. "I've been waiting for you to ask that."

"Really?"

"Yeah. Most people ask that question a lot sooner than you are now. It's a good question. I used to work as a tour guide for Skyview City Tours."

"Oh wow! I know all about them! You used to be a tour guide?"

"Yeah. I know this entire city like the back of my hand. I know the history behind every monument, street name, building, you name it. The only building I didn't know is The Agency building downtown. Other than that, I know everything about this place. I was giving a tour to a high school group. They were doing a tour and museum package. The group was rowdy and ghetto, mainly the boys. They were loud and weren't paying attention to a thing I was saying. I remember almost feeling sorry for their teacher or chaperone or whatever until I saw her on her phone talking on Facebook. Anyway, one of the boys in the group started to get loud with me as I was talking. I would say something about a particular landmark and he would repeat my words to mock me. He started to really get on my nerves. We have panic buttons on all of our tour buses but I didn't want to have the police come because a 17 year old kid was making fun of me. I tried to ignore him but he kept going. Finally I said something to him that embarrassed him. I called him out in front of his friends and that made him upset. We started to go back and forth until he literally stood up out of his chair to confront me. I would've beat the snot out that kid and sent him home to his mommy if all the other tourists on the bus didn't jump in between us and try to calm us down. I told the bus driver to take us back because I was done. I didn't want to deal with those kids anymore. The driver turns the bus to take us back. The other guests on the bus are now very upset because their tour is cut short. The teacher apologizes for the outburst while her student is still cursing me out and calling me all kinds of names. Long story short, we dropped the class off back where the tour starts. I then signal for the driver to drive off with the passengers that we had. We owed it to them to complete their tour. I did three more tours that day. When I got off work, I remember this like it was yesterday, the bus pulled in to the depot. The driver and I got off together like we always do. We locked the bus up and were talking about the game that night when I saw the kid that I got into the argument with. He was waiting for me. He was dark in the shadows but I recognized him right away. Before I could ask what he was doing there, he pulled out a gun and bam bam bam! I turned to run but I fell to the ground. I didn't realize but one of his shots shattered my knee. He had horrible aim and had the gun turned sideways. The bus driver ran off screaming and left me lying on the ground. The kid ran up and at close range, shot me point blank in the back of my head."

"Wow! Whatever happened to that kid? I ask.

"I don't know. I never knew his name so I can't look him up in our database. I simply remember falling, being in Hell, waking up to a Chief Presenter, and going to training."

"Man, I'm speechless. I'm so sorry."

"No need to be sorry about it now. That was a long time ago. Besides, you're nowhere near how sorry I am for dying and been given this choice. I wish I didn't have to face this reality in any capacity. Yet I do and I've embraced it." A moment of silence before Alexander fittingly ends the conversation. "It is what it is...and this chicken breast is awesome!"

"Good morning. My name is Sheila Williams and I'm your instructor for Positions in The Agency. This is your final class before you all receive your assignments. I wish to applaud all of you for making it this far. I don't know if any of you have been paying attention but this auditorium was full to capacity when you started classes three months ago. Now there are a few empty seats in the back."

Everyone turns around to look at the back of the room. I've been seated in the same seat for the past three months so I never noticed the seats behind me. There are empty seats. I never would've noticed. Sheila is right, some people aren't here. Sheila is a young African American woman. She doesn't look older than 35. She's beautiful. I wonder how she died and became a trainer.

"As you've all learned by now, this life isn't easy to live. Some people just can't cut it. It happens every time we add people to The Agency. To all of you seated here, you're one step closer to getting your assignment and it's our hope that you can maintain that for millenniums to come. What I'm assigned to teach you is the positions and divisions in The Agency. We teach this right before you receive your assignments because you're going to fall into one of these categories. You'll need to not only understand your assignment but also the hierarchy of your position. You may be in a support position and require further training. You may be in an interactive position and need resources from your Chief Presenter. You may become a Chief Presenter. You may become a Trainer. No matter what position you are assigned, it's your responsibility to understand and perform well. This will extend your time on Earth for as long as possible."

Sheila steps to the podium. She had been standing next to it to begin the class. She picks up a tablet that was resting on the podium and stands next to the podium again. If this was the beforelife, I would think that she is trying to showcase her body to the audience. She's wearing a fitted green dress with beige heels. Her beige belt matches perfectly. She has beads around her neck and her hair is styled in a very nice short cut.

"We start with the positions that you're already most familiar with and go from there. So the first position that some of you may receive as an assignment is the role of Chief Presenter. The Chief Presenter is the first person you met when you woke up in the afterlife. They probably gave you the shock of your life when you woke up from being in Hell." Sheila laughs but that's exactly what happened and it wasn't funny at all. Alexander scared me to death... but I was already dead. "The Chief Presenter's assignment is exactly what it sounds like. They are to present you to orientation and walk you through the process of training for your assignment. Depending on what your assignment is, your personal Chief Presenter may work with you to help you get acclimated. They will always be in an advisory role to assist you. You can always call upon your Chief Presenter. Consider them like a personal mentor. They can answer as many questions as you can ask. Each of them goes through a special training when they receive their assignment so they can answer your questions. They know everything. Think about your personal Chief Presenter and how many questions you've asked them. Did they ever respond that they didn't know the answer?"

She's absolutely right. Alexander has been great. I know I would've lost my mind in all of this afterlife stuff if it had not been for him. If I live on Earth for thousands of years, it is because of Alexander and I owe him for that.

Sheila continues reading from her tablet. "The Chief Presenter is the first line of introduction to the afterlife." She's now reading verbatim. "Their primary role is to disseminate information to the new inductee in a calm manner. It is the sole responsibility of the Chief Presenter that the new inductee graduates from the training program and accepts their assignment with The Agency." She looks up from her tablet. "If any of you is assigned as a Chief Presenter, you will learn a lot more of the details of the position."

I've thought of myself as a Chief Presenter several times. I think I would be perfect at it.

"There were two other people with the Chief Presenter when you met him or her. They were the security detail. These individuals in The Agency ensure the new inductee doesn't revolt against the Chief Presenter. They serve as drivers as well as security personnel."

Josh and Kevin were my security personnel and they feel more like brothers to me now. In a weird sense, I've started acclimating myself to this life. My new reality.

"The next set of individuals you came into contact with are trainers. Trainers are assigned with teaching you the four main courses for the afterlife on Earth. You've successfully completed the other three and this is the easiest one. Congratulations once again on making it this far. I hope that each of you has a long career with The Agency. I really hope we all have long careers! Training is an unusual position to be within The Agency because there are so many aspects to being a successful trainer. When I say success, I'm saying having the most students who turn out to be great members of The Agency. If I teach a class and every single person in the class fails their assignment, guess what happens to me? So I get nervous every time I come in here and see more than one empty seat." She makes a light hearted joke out of her last statement but I can tell she is very serious. "Training is designed to give out information in a way that won't frighten new inductees. We do a lot of things to distract you from what you're hearing as horrible news."

"You also met the Instructor Priest Dr. Reynolds. That's the next position. Instructor Priests deal with the spiritual training on angels and demons. They are well versed in the angelic realm and understand the history behind the spiritual conflict. Did you guys learn a lot from Dr. Reynolds?" Everyone claps. It's not a thunderous applause as if we were in a concert or a sporting event. It's more of a clap because she asked for acknowledgement. No one in this auditorium is happy so this unenthused clap is the best she's going to get.

Sheila puts her tablet back on the podium and stands behind it. She seems to become a little more serious as she continues. "Now for some of The Agency positions that you haven't heard of. These are individuals that new inductees never meet. Being a new inductee is overwhelming emotionally. It's a lot to take in to your heart and mind at the same time. Overloading you with information isn't smart when we at The Agency expect you to fulfill an important assignment. Therefore, we have carefully designed the amount of information that the human heart can receive without overloading. Having you meet more than the people you have met so far is mental overload based on anguish. We can't afford to do that as an organization and have expectations of success." She walks from behind the podium and slowly begins to walk from one side of the stage to the other. She casually places her arms behind her back as she paces. "Everything we do here at The Agency, to the smallest detail, is done on purpose. Nothing is by chance or coincidence. Everything is done with you guys, the new inductees in mind. Knowing how much you can handle, a lot of what we do in your orientation is based on distraction. Remember your first day of orientation? It was months ago but who remembers orientation?" She raises her hand to encourage each of us to raise our hands. Everyone in the auditorium raises their hand. "Good. Now who remembers the shape of the table in the middle of the orientation room? On the count of three, everyone scream the shape of the table. One... two... three!"

In unison, the entire audience says "Circle!"

"Right. The table in the middle of the orientation room is a circle. That table is a circle because studies have shown that humans will focus on the table and be distracted. Distracted from what? You were slightly distracted from the bad news that the Orientation Leader was sharing with you. Each of you focused on that table at least seven times if not more. At the least, seven times."

I'm amazed. I remember the circular table in the orientation room and I couldn't keep my eyes off of it. Who would've thought that it was a set-up to distract me? Have these people thought of everything?

"But back to my point. There are many members of The Agency that you have yet to meet and many you will never meet. I'll give brief descriptions of their roles as to make you aware. Throughout your time with The Agency, you will come to know these positions and responsibilities as second nature. First is the Governing Magistrate. These people have been trained to manage certain areas and regions throughout the world. There is a Governing Magistrate who covers North America for example. This person's assignment is to make sure that the plans that are decided by the Advisory Council are set in motion. The job is extremely detailed. For example, if one of you has the assignment of becoming a trainer and you consistently have students who fail their assignment, you will wind up in Hell. Bottom line. If enough trainers in North America experience the same fate, the Regional Director and all the way up the ladder to the Governing Magistrate will suffer the same fate. Therefore, each position in The Agency takes their position seriously. If not... you know the rest."

"Since I just mentioned The Advisory Council, let's talk about them next. These are members of The Agency that you will never meet. They send directives for each region. If there is a decision to build a new facility, that directive comes from The Advisory Council. The decision as to who is invited to become a member of The Agency comes from The Council. There are hundreds of thousands of people who can potentially die tomorrow. The people selected to come back to work for The Agency are carefully selected from all that die. Your selection is important as it is key to the assignment you will be given and to your success in that assignment. You should consider yourselves very fortunate to be sitting in this room."

Based on how a person looks at things, she could be very right. Sitting in this room means you're going to face and endure the worst fate known to man. Sitting in this room means you have delayed the worst fate known to man for possibly thousands of years. Finding the balance between the two is incredibly difficult to live with. I wholeheartedly agree with her though as I would rather be in this room than the alternative.

"The final position I want to mention to you is the Area Principle Director. This person is the boss of all Chief Presenters. You will meet him at the end of this course. He is the person who makes sure all the training of Chief Presenters goes well and presents the new inductees with their assignments. He will deliver a State of The Agency address and then the closing part of the ceremony will be the giving out of assignments. Each of you will have three people with you at your assignment ceremony; your Chief Presenter and both of your security personnel."

"Ceremony?" I lean to my right and whisper into Ferdinand's ear. Ferdinand has sat next to me for each of the sessions held in this auditorium. Everyone sits in the same seat so you're almost forced to get to know the person on the left and right of you. Ferdinand died of a heart attack at a very young age. He was only 47. Seated to my left is Barry. Like me, he died in a car accident but the major difference with him is that he wasn't alone. His wife was with him in the car and she also died in the accident. His anguish is that he is now a member of The Agency and he believes his wife avoided The Agency and Hell by getting into Heaven. According to Barry's Chief Presenter, there is no way to know for certain. They can only verify members of The Agency, past and present. Barry now must live his afterlife and work his assignment never knowing what happened to his wife of seven years.

"They do everything big with this Agency bro! Yuri told me that they have a ceremony like a graduation and people are clapping for you when you go up to get your assignment packet!" Yuri is Ferdinand's Chief Presenter. Ferdinand told me all about him as I told Ferdinand all about Alexander. I started to recognize how large The Agency is when I found out that Alexander and Yuri were both Chief Presenters in the same District, working out of the same building but had never met and didn't know of one another. When I asked Alexander about Yuri over dinner one night, he told me he had never met him. There are so many Chief Presenters, there's no way to know each of them. They are merely coworkers in a humongous organization. "He said this guy gets up and gives an address like a real graduation!"

"Wow. This place never ceases to amaze me." I reply.

"All to keep you motivated right?"

"Right."

Dinner in my home tonight is seared tenderloin with mustard horseradish sauce served on baguette slices topped with capes, olive oil and parmesan cheese. Exquisite as usual. The food from The Agency never disappoints. Last night we had pan seared sesame salmon with miso slaw, fried rice and chocolate wontons.

"What can you tell me about the guy who gives the speech and hands out the assignments?" I ask Alexander during our routine question and answer time during dinner.

"Oh Mr. Weincaster. His name is Mitchell Weincaster. He's the guy who is over my position. Wait til you hear him speak. He's dynamic!" Alexander says.

"Oh yeah?"
"Yeah, he's a dynamic speaker. He was a motivational speaker in his beforelife and he was very good. He ran several businesses before he died so he is a proven leader. The position that he's accepted with The Agency fits his personality perfectly. He gets to lead a large team of people and every semester he speaks to the graduating inductees. Let me tell you, you will be ultra-motivated to do your assignment when he's finished... whatever your assignment is!"

"I think some of us are gonna need all the motivation we can get!" I say.

"Trust me when I tell you. When you receive your assignment, you'll be more than ready to be the best member of The Agency in the history of The Agency. Believe that my brother!"

"How did you feel when you got your assignment?" I ask.

Alexander pauses before he answers. He seems to think about his answer before he answers. "I was relieved. I was scared but I knew that no matter what, I had to work my assignment. I was more focused and dedicated than ever. I knew that I was cut out to be a Chief Presenter. I knew I would never fail a new inductee. I set out to dominate this position and make sure every new inductee I would become assigned to would succeed!"

"Yeah but that's covering your own ass! I mean come on, be real with me! If I fail, you go to Hell too! This ain't got nothing to do with a new inductee! This is all about you!"

"Brian, the entire point of working your assignment is self-preservation first and working your assignment second! If you've learned nothing from these classes and from me through all of this you should've at least learned that!" Alexander matches my tone and volume with his response. He's right. My outburst is a result of my extreme fear of what's ahead and the notion that I may not be able to complete my assignment. Not that I'm not confident in my personal skills but what if I'm a Chief Presenter and I get a new inductee like Frank? Frank couldn't handle the pressure so he went back to Hell and so did his Chief Presenter. Therefore, of course Alexander wants me to do well so the same doesn't happen to him because of me.

"Look. I'm assigned to you. That's for the entire afterlife. As long as you're with The Agency, I got your back. Whatever you need, I'm here for you okay? It can be ten years from now and I'm still here with you. That's my assignment as your CP and that's my commitment to you. We have to succeed man. We have to."

I take a moment before I speak. I simply look back at him. Alexander has been with me every single day since I woke up on this side of life. He's answered every question I've had and even let me cry in front of him. He's a great Chief Presenter and mentor and I hope to be as good as him when I get assigned. "You're right man. I'm just nervous about my assignment. That's all."

"That's fine. That's natural. We all were. Whatever your assignment is, it was specifically set up for you based on what The Council knows you can do. I was assigned as a CP because they knew I would be good at it. So don't worry. Just be yourself and you'll be fine. Your assignment is for you based on you."

"Don't worry. Yeah right." I laugh a little which breaks the tense moment.

Alexander smiles and puts his hand on my shoulder. "You'll do fine man. You might want to go to bed a little early. Tomorrow is a huge day."

"I don't think I'm gonna be able to sleep tonight." I say.

"Yes you will."

I open my eyes and I'm in Hell! What happened? Why am I... Someone pushes me from behind and I fall to the ground. Before I realize what's happening, a group of people tumble on top of me and they are all on fire as I am. I'm in incredible paid and I scream out. The ground underneath me is the hottest thing I've ever touched! I feel like someone just pushed my entire body on top of a burning grill! Everyone is moving and screaming! I scream out as the people on top of me wiggle their way out of this tumbled pile. As soon as I get to my feet, I look around at the horror that surrounds me. There is fire everywhere and my entire body is burning. Before I can even ask what happened to me, I see a monster that looks like a cherubim described in my class. He's got both a man and a woman in his grasp, one in each hand. They are screaming and crying, both on fire. He looks at me and we make direct eye contact. Out of the huge crowd of people screaming around me, he sees me. He throws each of the people he is holding like rag dolls. The woman goes flying, screaming as she lands in the lake that looks like red lava. There are so many people in the lake that its hard to see where she lands but they're all trying to get out of it. It's burning each one of them severely. I don't see where the man was thrown to but the cherubim starts to push through people to get to me! I turn and try to run away but the crowd of people around me reminds me of Time Square during New Year's Eve times one hundred! Everyone is on fire and screaming! People are pushing and shoving and falling over one another. I'm screaming because I'm in so much pain and I don't know how I got here!

"Alexander! Alexander! Help me! Somebody help me! Why am I here! I never got my assignme..."

The cherubim grabs me from behind! His hands are so big and his grasp is so tight that I can't breathe. He's on fire and seemingly in pain as I am but his goal right now is to hurt me. He forgoes his own torture in order to inflict pain upon me! He slams me to the ground and picks me back up. That hit was so hard it felt like every bone in my body broke. My head hit so hard that I'm dizzy. He slams me down a second time and I wish I could die but I'm already dead and in Hell. I don't understand what happened. Why did I come here? I didn't give up on my assignment! I didn...

Before I can think he tosses me like he did the people he had before me. He sets his sights on someone else and goes for them. I fall into a burning pit of fire and am engulfed in flames. I scream and cry but I can't even hear my own voice. There is so much screaming, yelling and crying. It smells like the worst garbage dump I've ever been around.

I climb out of the pit of fire and crawl across the ground. There's nowhere to go. There's nowhere to hide. I'm in Hell forever and am burning... dead... in pain... on fire... screaming forev...

I pop up in my bed screaming. This time I'm so shocked that I fall out of the bed and knock my lamp onto the floor. The lamp shatters as it hits the hard wood floor. I'm so disoriented and afraid that I scream at the sound. My lights turn on and Alexander and Kevin are seated in my bedroom.

"What just happened! What just happened!" I scream out. I'm crying profusely and looking at Alexander for some kind of response.

"Brian calm down. Get your breath. Calm do..."

"What just happened to me! Was that a dream? Was that real?" I scream again. I think I'm going into a panic shock.

"That was your final dream. Everyone visits Hell in their dreams the night before they get their assignment. That's why we're here, to talk to you about it."

"What! Why? Why!"

"Because you're getting your assignment today." He says. "The Agency reminds you of the consequence of not taking your assignment. If your assignment is particularly difficult or something you don't want to do, The Agency reminds you one last time of the alternative. Whatever your assignment is, if you choose to not accept it, you go to Hell and you cannot come back. They send each new inductee to Hell in their dreams to give them one final incentive to accept their assignment."

I'm so stunned that I don't know what to say.

"You okay?"

"Was that necessary! Dammit man!" I yell back at him. I look at the broken lamp on the floor then back at Alexander and Kevin. "And what you doing here! Y'all think I'm gonna go crazy and attack Alexander or something?" I direct my anger toward Kevin. "Is security really necessary?"

"It's happened." Alexander says. "Chief Presenters have been attacked right after final dreams. Having security is only a precautionary measure."

I start to get up off the floor and Kevin gets up to help me. As soon as he touches me to help, I push him away. "Don't touch me!" I sit on the side of the bed and put my face into my hands. I begin to cry so hard that I can feel my entire body heaving. No one says anything. Both Alexander and Kevin allow me to have my heavy cry.

"We're going downstairs to let you get showered and dressed. You won't be able to go back to sleep so you might as well jump in the shower and start to get ready to get your assignment. It's almost 6:00 am anyway."

I don't take my head out of my hands but I hear Alexander. I'm still crying heavily when I hear them get up to leave my bedroom.

"If it makes you feel any better, every new inductee experiences this dream. Right at this very moment, there are Chief Presenters all over the place sitting with crying new inductees. You all were in the same dream at the same time. Now is your recovery time to get yourself together. Take a long shower and we'll see you downstairs by 8:00 am." At that, I hear them leave my bedroom and close the door.

The State of The Agency address is being held in a different building. For the first time since I arrived at The Agency training facility, I'm being escorted to a meeting somewhere else. There is a convention center in the heart of town and that's where Josh drives us. Alexander said that we had to be here by 9:00 am and it's not even 7:45 am yet when we pull up. As we arrive, I notice there are others with the same idea of being early. There are hundreds of cars already in the parking lot and even more people walking toward the convention center from their cars.

"Wow, I thought we would be the first ones here." I say.

"No." Alexander replies. "Every new inductee is going to be arriving early. Studies have shown that none of us can go back to sleep after the dream and the anxiousness to receive the assignment. Every time we do this, people are here very early. They wake up from the dream, they shake violently and cry their eyes out, they get dressed and they come get their assignments. Happens all the time."

"Why is this being done here and not in the regular building?" I ask as Josh parks the SUV.

"This is literally set up like a graduation. Every new inductee that made it to this point is going to be here. Every Chief Presenter for those inductees as well all security. Every trainer that you've had, basically everybody. A larger venue is needed for this. This is a huge event every time we do it."

We get out of the truck and join the crowd walking toward the coliseum. This place holds thousands of people at a time and it looks like the size is going to be applicable to the crowd. As much as I've learned over the past few months about life, humanity and The Agency, I still find myself amazed with all of this. So many people are here to find out what will delay them from going to Hell immediately. We hate it and love it at the same time. This is absolutely amazing to me. I watch people of all races walking in and filling rows of seats. I see both Suzanne and Sheldon along with their Chief Presenters and security team. I see Ferdinand and Barry with both of their Chief Presenters and security. I see familiar faces from the classes I took. I follow Josh who leads us to the ground level where we approach a roped-off area.

"Okay man. Only new inductees can go through here. All of you will be seated on the ground level, we will be on level two. After you hear the keynote address, meet us right over there." Alexander points to an area to the left of the main stage. I'll have your assignment in an envelope by then and I'll let you open it and read it."

"The anxiousness is killing me man!" I say.

"I know. We all been there but look, I'm proud of you Brian. We're all very proud of you. You did well and I hope you're with The Agency for one hundred thousand times one hundred thousand years."

"Alright man. You're on your own now. Enjoy the speech and I'll see you at the end of the event and give you your assignment!"

"Ladies and gentlemen! Please rise for the entrance of our Area Principle Director, The Honorable Dr. Mitchell Weincaster!" A voice over a loud surround-sound system announces the keynote speaker and everyone in the second and third levels rises to their feet to applaud loudly. New inductees on the first level rise too. The new inductees don't know what to do. Since the Chief Presenters, trainers and security members all stand and clap, we follow suit.

I notice everyone looking behind us and I turn to see what is happening back there. There is a procession of people walking toward the stage. I already see Dr. Weincaster. He definitely stands out. He is tall, at least 6 feet 7 inches. He has on a blue suit with a sharp white shirt and polka dot blue tie. He has a white carnation flower in the lapel of his jacket. I can tell by the way he walks that he is used to being in charge and has the confidence of a lion among lambs. He is surrounded by a team of people who look like a mix of college professors and security. As he steps onto the stage, he waves at the audience and the applause heightens. This man is a celebrity within The Agency and he receives all the love that is being poured out to him. He approaches the podium and goes from one raised hand waving to two raised hands lifted. He smiles to the left and right and everyone continues to clap and scream. He motions for the crowd to take their seats but the applause continues. He steps back from the podium and speaks into the ear of one of the men who walked in with him. They both laugh before he steps back to the podium. This time he leans forward to speak into the microphone.

"Thank you! Thank you! Please, take your seats!" His voice is as deep as it should seem for a man of his stature. Everyone takes their seats. "Good morning members of The

Agency!" He booms his morning declaration so loudly that everyone in the second and third levels rises and applauds again. New inductees follow as we don't want to do anything wrong. The Honorable Dr. Weincaster steps back from the podium to receive the second round of applause. Once he steps forward again, he beams a smile as big as his personality. He motions for everyone to sit again.

"So how did everyone sleep last night?" Everyone in attendance bursts into laughter except for the new inductees. Clearly this is a joke on the new inductees as according to Alexander, we each experienced the same horrific dream last night. "I'm kidding, I'm kidding. To the new inductees, that's a little joke that I say each time I give this speech as a means to lighten the tension a little. Everyone in this filled to capacity arena is in the same situation and has decided in his or her own best interest to make the best of it. What happened to you last night happened to all of us. Each and every one of us at one point. We were all new inductees at one time or another. We've however made a decision that I hope each of you new members make as well. We decided to work as hard as we can at whatever we do to never go back until we absolutely have to. You don't have to worry about performing your assignment well. The Agency hand selected you based on your beforelife to perform exceptional in your afterlife. You will do well! We have faith in you and we believe in you! Do not be afraid! Working your assignment will prove to be the best decision you will ever make! Let me share with you some assignment success stories!"

Immediately five people that walked in with him stand up. They are seated behind him on the stage. One of the men he whispered to a moment ago is one of the five that stands. The rest of the people behind him look more like a security detail fit for the President of the United States.

"I want to introduce you to five Agency success stories. They will each come up, give their name, and let you know how long they have been with The Agency."

The man that he whispered to a few minutes ago steps to the microphone as Dr. Weincaster steps to the side. He is a middle age White man. "Hello my name is Thomas and I've been working various assignments for The Agency for three hundred and thirteen years." The audience begins a thunderous applause but he steps back as if he said something very common. I'm in shock as I continue to listen.

The next person steps to the podium and speaks. "Hi my name is Ashley and as of this July, I've been with The Agency six hundred years!" The applause continues, seemingly stronger for Ashley, an African American woman, than for Thomas.

"My name is Patricia and I've been with The Agency for nine hundred and seventy-one years!"

This is unbelievable! Almost one thousand years?

"Hello, my name is Kirk. I've been on with The Agency for eleven hundred and twenty two years and I want to do eleven hundred and twenty-two more times five!" Kirk's response draws laughter with applause.

Before the final person speaks, Dr. Weincaster leans to the microphone. "Eleven hundred and twenty-two years! He looks great for his age doesn't he?" The audience, and now the new inductees laugh. With each person who has spoken thus far, the new inductees gasp with surprise. This guy just said he died over one thousand years ago! I can't even imagine how he's adjusted to living through some of the historic things that have happened in the last one thousand years! Things I learned in history classes in high school he may have witnessed firsthand. I'm absolutely stunned.

The final person steps to the podium. A woman who looks to be of Hispanic descent. "Hello Agency!" The Chief Presenters and Trainers all respond with a loud hello. "To the new inductees, my name is Ava and I have been with The Agency for two thousand seven hundred and three years!" With that, everyone in the two tiers of the convention center rises to their feet with a thunderous applause. New inductees quickly follow. Ava smiles as she steps back to her seat.

Dr. Weincaster returns to the middle of the podium with a big smile on his face. His right hand is in the air as he begins. "Raise your hand if you want to work for The Agency as long as Ms. Ava!" Everyone in the building raises their hand as the Chief Presenters and trainers take their seats. "We welcome you to The Agency. We would like for each of you to maintain a long career with us for as long as you can. When you get your assignments today, embrace them. Work them. Succeed in them. Move through the ranks of The Agency if you can. Do all that you can to avoid what you can. There's a good chance that you can live on Earth for one million millenniums! We all want that. It's up to you to get it."

"There are many things you may not have gotten to

do in your beforelife that you can now. There may be areas in your career development that you never had the opportunity to pursue. There may be creative ideas you've had and never had the chance to express them. Express them now. The reason The Agency has been able to flourish for as many years as it has is because of people like you and I who bring these ideas and expertise to the table. Help us help you! Help us to build an organization that will sustain its millions of members for as long as possible! The Agency needs you! I hope you need it as well!"

He changes his tone as he continues. "I'm going to tell you a story. I met a young man who had come into The Agency about thirteen or so years ago. At that time I was in a department called The Discovery Team. My job back then was to look at a person's background and help decide what their assignment was going to be. When I met this young man face to face, I immediately recognized him because we had just gone through his files a few days prior. I approached him to say hello and he was looking down. He was depressed over his situation. He was thinking about his beforelife and all that he had lost in death. He was thinking about going to Hell and experiencing that pain. He thought about the fire and the liquid lake. The demons and all the screaming. That made him depressed. I tried to encourage him and cheer him up. I wasn't allowed to share with him what his assignment was but I knew it was something he would be able to do. It was hand selected for him and it would have been a wonderful situation to be in. The Agency was setting him up in a political environment where he would one day be a governor. He would be afforded luxuries beyond what he could imagine and he would win the elections he had to run." He pauses before he continues his story. He takes a long pause. He rubs his chin as if he is considering the depth of the story he is sharing. He continues. "I wish I could have shared with him the great assignment that was hand selected for him. Before he received his assignment, he caved under the pressure and left The Agency." Weincaster pauses to allow that to sink in. He continues. "That was thirteen years ago. Had he stayed with the course and accepted his assignment, he would have been a name that you all would be familiar with today. Yet he has been in torment now for thirteen years. He regrets it every minute. Don't be that guy. Stay the course and work your assignment!"

Alexander was absolutely correct about Dr. Weincaster. He knows how to motivate a crowd. That was a very moving story. Not so much in the story itself but simply how Dr. Weincaster told it. He knew when to pause and when to smile. He knew when to speak louder and when to speak as soft as a whisper. He's an expert and even I am encouraged based on that story.

The Agency seems to be well equipped with motivating its members. Avoiding hell should be motivation enough but people have a variety of personality traits. That may be a good avoidance for me but not necessarily for someone else. It wasn't enough for Frank. Some people may need to hear a story like this in order to be motivated. Some needed the final dream from last night. Whatever the motivation, The Agency takes no shorts in ensuring the loyalty of its millions of members. Whatever assignments are handed out in the next few minutes will be worked completely by every new inductee here. I'm more than certain of that.

"I wish each of you much success! I wish you as many years as these Agency success stories that you just heard from! I wish to thank each of your Chief Presenters! I salute you!" He waves toward the upper tiers of the arena. "To your trainers, I salute you all! Thank you for the hard work that you do to make all our lives a little more comfortable! To all of the security detail, I salute you!" He waves at the security in the audience and the team behind him before he returns to face the new inductees. "Now let's get out there and work our assignments!"

With that, Dr. Weincaster steps back from the podium to a standing ovation. Amidst all the clapping and cheering, I know that every new inductee is as anxious as I am to receive our assignments. Whatever my assignment is, I hope I have it for ten million years. I want to be on stage behind a keynote speaker and awe the audience with how long I've been on Earth after my death.

Another man steps to the microphone as the applause begins to dwindle for Dr. Weincaster. He is a much shorter man and has to bend the microphone down in order to speak into it. "Thank you Dr. Weincaster for those stirring words. You always encourage us toward the bettering of our future and we thank you." Everyone takes their seats. "To the new inductees, you have successfully completed your courses here at The Agency and we congratulate you. Now is the time you've all been waiting for. We know each of you is anxious to find out what your assignment is and we don't wish to delay you any further. Your Chief Presenter was given an envelope while Dr. Weincaster was speaking. Inside that envelope is your assignment. Your Chief Presenter gave you instructions as to where to meet him or her after this ceremony. It is now after the ceremony. Feel free to get your assignment! Congratulations!"

Before the word congratulations leaves his lips, a new inductee seated toward the front leaps up and starts to make his way toward his Chief Presenter. With that, everyone gets up and begins quickly moving. It's like mayhem as we're all desperately trying to get to our CP. For the first time since being introduced to The Agency, it seems as if there is total chaos. Everything with The Agency is well organized and structured. Now the new inductees are running and almost falling over one another to get their assignment. I am as well.

Alexander, Kevin and Josh are smiling as I approach. Kevin is actually laughing at me. I find no humor yet his laughter causes me to laugh as well. "So, you ready to get your assignment?" Alexander is waving my envelope from side to side as he speaks to me with a smile.

"Stop playing with me!" I say smiling but with all seriousness.

"Here you go. Be careful opening it, I don't want you to tear the letter in half!" Alexander hands me the envelope. I turn it over. The envelope is sealed with The Agency logo and is signed across the seal by Dr. Weincaster. I assume that is to ensure that the envelope hasn't been opened by none other than the intended new inductee. I carefully break the seal and take out the folded paper. I drop the envelope onto the floor.

"Read it out loud." Alexander says.

"From The Council of..." I skip that part. "Dear Mr. Brian Lampkin. It is indeed our pleasure to welcome you as a new member of The Agency. We are proud that you have decided to prolong your stay on Earth and work along with our dedicated team. It is our intent that you have a long career with us and we hope that is your intent as well. Once again, on behalf of the entire Council and all the members of The Agency, welcome."

I read the next paragraph out loud as well. "Your assignment. You are to meet Angela Renee Hamilton. She is a single, twenty-seven year old African American female. She has been praying earnestly for a husband. We have purposely designed you to be the husband she has been asking God for. Your assignment is to meet Ms. Hamilton and cause her to fall in love with you. You will ask Ms. Hamilton to marry you, making her Mrs. Angela Renee Lampkin. You are then to ensure that Mrs. Angela Renee Lampkin, all of your children with her and all of your grandchildren with her go to Hell."

I look up from the letter and stare at Alexander. He seems speechless. I look back at the letter to make sure I read correctly what I just read out loud. I look up again and back at Alexander. "Wait... what?"

THE ASSIGNMENT TWO:
KEEP YOUR ENEMIES CLOSER

Coming July 19th, 2018

ASSIGNMENT
TWO

KEEP YOUR ENEMIES CLOSER

DARRIUS JEROME GOURDINE

THANK YOU

Thank you Father God for the gifts of life and writing. Thank you Jesus for saving my soul. Thank you Holy Spirit for guiding me daily and for helping me navigate the writing of this book. Thank you Kathy Gourdine for always supporting my writing career. I love you. Thank you Paul Woodruff for your amazing design skills in producing the cover and artwork for this project. Thank you to Norman Rich for the layout and praying for me at least for the next few weeks! (smile) Thank you James McDuffie for your awesome photography skills. Thank you to my three story proofreaders, Rev. Lynnette Daughtry Barrett, Kenya Marie Farmer, and Brooke Harris. I appreciate each of you for your honest feedback and words of encouragement. Thank you to each person who took the time to read this book. I pray you enjoyed it and are looking forward to more works from me.

Thank you to my son Dylan Joshua Gourdine. You don't realize it yet, but all of my late night writing binges are for you. I love you more than any words I could ever type in any book.

God bless you all!

Darrius Jerome

Made in the USA
Columbia, SC
23 January 2018